Charles Dickens, Adelaide Anne Procter

Legends and Lyrics

A Book of Verses

Charles Dickens, Adelaide Anne Procter

Legends and Lyrics
A Book of Verses

ISBN/EAN: 9783744777391

Printed in Europe, USA, Canada, Australia, Japan

Cover: Foto ©Andreas Hilbeck / pixelio.de

More available books at **www.hansebooks.com**

LEGENDS AND LYRICS

A BOOK OF VERSES

BY ADELAIDE ANNE PROCTER

WITH AN INTRODUCTION BY

CHARLES DICKENS

LONDON:

GEORGE BELL & SONS, YORK ST., COVENT GARDEN,

AND NEW YORK.

1892.

CROWN 8VO EDITION.

*First published May, 1881. Reprinted Dec. 1881,
1883, 1884, 1885, 1887, 1892.*

CONTENTS.

Contents.

Contents.

Contents.

AN INTRODUCTION.

BY CHARLES DICKENS.

N the spring of the year 1853, I observed, as Conductor of the Weekly Journal HOUSEHOLD WORDS, a short poem among the proffered contributions, very different, as I thought, from the shoal of verses perpetually setting through the office of such a Periodical, and possessing much more merit. Its authoress was quite unknown to me. She was one MISS MARY BERWICK, whom I had never heard of; and she was to be addressed by letter, if addressed at all, at a circulating library in the western district of London. Through this channel, Miss Berwick was informed that her poem was accepted, and was invited to send another. She complied, and became a regular and frequent contributor. Many letters passed between the Journal and Miss Berwick, but Miss Berwick herself was never seen.

How we came gradually to establish, at the office of Household Words, that we knew all about Miss Berwick, I have never discovered. But, we settled somehow, to our complete satisfaction, that she was governess in a family; that she went to Italy in that capacity, and returned; and that she had long been in the same family. We really knew nothing whatever of her, except that she was remarkably business-like, punctual, self-reliant, and reliable : so I suppose we insensibly invented the rest. For myself, my mother was not a more real personage to me, than Miss Berwick the governess became.

This went on until December, 1854, when the Christmas Number, entitled, The Seven Poor Travellers, was sent to press. Happening to be going to dine that day with an old and dear friend, distinguished in literature as BARRY CORNWALL, I took with me an early proof of that Number, and remarked, as I laid it on the drawing-room table, that it contained a very pretty poem, written by a certain Miss Berwick. Next day brought me the disclosure that I had so spoken of the poem to the mother of its writer, in its writer's presence; that I had no such correspondent in existence as Miss Berwick; and that the name had been assumed by Barry Cornwall's eldest daughter, MISS ADELAIDE ANNE PROCTER.

The anecdote I have here noted down, besides serving to explain why the parents of the late Miss Procter have looked to me for these poor words of remembrance of their lamented child, strikingly illustrates the honesty, independence, and quiet dignity, of the lady's character. I had known her when she was very young; I had been honoured with her father's friendship when I was myself a young aspirant; and she had said at home, "If I send him, in my own name, verses that he does not honestly like, either it will be very painful to him to return them, or he will print them for papa's sake, and not for their own. So I have made up my mind to take my chance fairly with the unknown volunteers."

Perhaps it requires an Editor's experience of the profoundly unreasonable grounds on which he is often urged to accept unsuitable articles—such as having been to school with the writer's husband's brother-in-law, or having lent an alpenstock in Switzerland to the writer's wife's nephew, when that interesting stranger had broken his own—fully to appreciate the delicacy and the self-respect of this resolution.

Some verses by Miss Procter had been published in the BOOK OF BEAUTY, ten years before she became Miss Berwick. With the exception of two poems in the CORNHILL MAGAZINE, two in GOOD WORDS, and others in a little book called A CHAPLET OF VERSES (issued in 1862 for the benefit of a Night Refuge), her published writings first appeared in HOUSEHOLD WORDS, or ALL THE YEAR ROUND. The present Edition contains the whole of her Legends and Lyrics, and originates in the great favour with which they have been received by the public.

Miss Procter was born in Bedford-square, London,

on the 30th of October, 1825. Her love of poetry was conspicuous at so early an age, that I have before me a tiny album made of small note-paper, into which her favourite passages were copied for her by her mother's hand before she herself could write. It looks as if she had carried it about, as another little girl might have carried a doll. She soon displayed a remarkable memory, and great quickness of apprehension. When she was quite a young child, she learnt with facility several of the problems of Euclid. As she grew older, she acquired the French, Italian, and German, languages; became a clever piano-forte player; and showed a true taste and sentiment in drawing. But, as soon as she had completely vanquished the difficulties of any one branch of study, it was her way to lose interest in it, and pass to another. While her mental resources were being trained, it was not at all suspected in her family that she had any gift of authorship, or any ambition to become a writer. Her father had no idea of her having ever attempted to turn a rhyme, until her first little poem saw the light in print.

When she attained to womanhood, she had read an extraordinary number of books, and throughout her life she was always largely adding to the number. In 1853 she went to Turin and its neighbourhood, on a visit to her aunt, a Roman Catholic lady. As Miss Procter had herself professed the Roman Catholic Faith two years before, she entered with the greater ardour on the study of the Piedmontese dialect, and the observation of the habits and manners of the peasantry.

In the former, she soon became a proficient. On the latter head, I extract from her familiar letters written home to England at the time, two pleasant pieces of description.

A Betrothal.

" We have been to a ball, of which I must give you a description. Last Tuesday we had just done dinner at about seven, and stepped out into the balcony to look at the remains of the sunset behind the mountains, when we heard very distinctly a band of music, which rather excited my astonishment, as a solitary organ is the utmost that toils up here. I went out of the room for a few minutes, and, on my returning, Emily said, ' Oh ! That band is playing at the farmer's near here. The daughter is *fiancée* to-day, and they have a ball.' I said, ' I wish I was going ! ' ' Well,' replied she, ' the farmer's wife did call to invite us.' ' Then, I shall certainly go,' I exclaimed. I applied to Madame B., who said she would like it very much, and we had better go, children and all. Some of the servants were already gone. We rushed away to put on some shawls, and put off any shred of black we might have about us (as the people would have been quite annoyed if we had appeared on such an occasion with any black), and we started. When we reached the farmer's, which is a stone's throw above our house, we were received with great enthusiasm ; the only drawback being, that no one spoke French, and we did not yet speak Pied-montese. We were placed on a bench against the wall,

b

and the people went on dancing. The room was a large whitewashed kitchen (I suppose), with several large pictures in black frames, and very smoky. I distinguished the Martyrdom of Saint Sebastian, and the others appeared equally lively and appropriate subjects. Whether they were Old Masters or not, and if so, by whom, I could not ascertain. The band were seated opposite us. Five men, with wind instruments, part of the band of the National Guard, to which the farmer's sons belong. They played really admirably, and I began to be afraid that some idea of our dignity would prevent my getting a partner; so, by Madame B.'s advice, I went up to the bride, and offered to dance with her. Such a handsome young woman! Like one of Uwins's pictures. Very dark, with a quantity of black hair, and on an immense scale. The children were already dancing, as well as the maids. After we came to an end of our dance, which was what they call a Polka-Mazourka, I saw the bride trying to screw up the courage of her *fiancé* to ask me to dance, which after a little hesitation he did. And admirably he danced, as indeed they all did—in excellent time, and with a little more spirit than one sees in a ball room. In fact, they were very like one's ordinary partners, except that they wore ear-rings and were in their shirt-sleeves, and truth compels me to state that they decidedly smelt of garlic. Some of them had been smoking, but threw away their cigars when we came in. The only thing that did not look cheerful was, that the room was only lighted by two or three oil-lamps, and that there seemed to be no preparation for refreshments. Madame B., seeing this, whispered to her maid, who disengaged herself from her partner, and ran off to the house; she and the kitchenmaid presently returning with a large tray covered with all kinds of cakes (of which we are great consumers and always have a stock), and a large hamper full of bottles of wine, with coffee and sugar. This seemed all very acceptable. The *fiancée* was requested to distribute the eatables, and a bucket of water being produced to wash the glasses in, the wine disappeared very quickly—as fast as they could open the bottles. But, elated I suppose by this, the floor was sprinkled with water, and the musicians played a Monferrino, which is a Piedmontese dance. Madame B. danced with the farmer's son, and Emily with another distinguished member of the company. It was very fatiguing—something like a Scotch reel. My partner was a little man, like Perrot, and very proud of his dancing. He cut in the air and twisted about, until I was out of breath, though my attempts to imitate him were feeble in the extreme. At last, after seven or eight dances, I was obliged to sit down. We stayed till nine, and I was so dead beat with the heat that I could hardly crawl about the house, and in an agony with the cramp, it is so long since I have danced."

A Marriage.

"The wedding of the farmer's daughter has taken place. We had hoped it would have been in the little chapel of our house, but it seems some special permission was necessary, and they applied for it too late They all said, 'This is the Constitution. There would have been no difficulty before!' the lower classes making the poor Constitution the scape-goat for everything they don't like. So as it was impossible for us to climb up to the church where the wedding was to be, we contented ourselves with seeing the procession pass. It was not a very large one, for, it requiring some activity to go up, all the old people remained at home. It is not the etiquette for the bride's mother to go, and no unmarried woman can go to a wedding—I suppose for fear of its making her discontented with her own position. The procession stopped at our door, for the bride to receive our congratulations. She was dressed in a shot silk, with a yellow handkerchief, and rows of a large gold chain. In the afternoon they sent to request us to go there. On our arrival we found them dancing out of doors, and a most melancholy affair it was. All the bride's sisters were not to be recognized, they had cried so. The mother sat in the house, and could not appear. And the bride was sobbing so, she could hardly stand! The most melancholy spectacle of all to my mind, was, that the bridegroom was decidedly tipsy. He seemed rather affronted at all the distress. We danced a Monferrino; I with the bridegroom; and the bride crying the whole time. The company did their utmost to enliven her by firing pistols, but without success, and at last they began a series of yells, which reminded me of a set of savages. But even this delicate

method of consolation failed, and the wishing good-bye
began.   It was altogether so melancholy an affair that
Madame B. dropped a few tears, and I was very near
it, particularly when the poor mother came out to see
the last of her daughter, who was finally dragged off
between her brother and uncle, with a last explosion of
pistols.   As she lives quite near, makes an excellent
match, and is one of nine children, it really was a most
desirable marriage, in spite of all this show of distress.
Albert was so discomfited by it, that he forgot to kiss
the bride as he had intended to do, and therefore went
to call upon her yesterday, and found her very smiling
in her new house, and supplied the omission.   The
cook came home from the wedding, declaring she was
cured of any wish to marry—but I would not recommend
any man to act upon that threat and make her an offer.
In a couple of days we had some rolls of the bride's
first baking, which they call Madonnas.   The musicians,
it seems, were in the same state as the bridegroom, for,
in escorting her home, they all fell down in the mud.
My wrath against the bridegroom is somewhat calmed
by finding that it is considered bad luck if he does not
get tipsy at his wedding."

Those readers of Miss Procter's poems who should
suppose from their tone that her mind was of a gloomy
or despondent cast, would be curiously mistaken.   She
was exceedingly humorous, and had a great delight in
humour.   Cheerfulness was habitual with her, she was
very ready at a sally or a reply, and in her laugh (as I
remember well) there was an unusual vivacity, enjoy-

ment, and sense of drollery. She was perfectly uncon-
strained and unaffected : as modestly silent about her
productions, as she was generous with their pecuniary
results. She was a friend who inspired the strongest
attachments ; she was a finely sympathetic woman, with
a great accordant heart and a sterling noble nature.
No claim can be set up for her, thank God, to the
possession of any of the conventional poetical qualities.
She never by any means held the opinion that she was
among the greatest of human beings ; she never suspected the existence of a conspiracy on the part of
mankind against her ; she never recognized in her best
friends, her worst enemies ; she never cultivated the
luxury of being misunderstood and unappreciated ; she
would far rather have died without seeing a line of her
composition in print, than that I should have maundered
about her, here, as "the Poet," or "the Poetess."

With the recollection of Miss Procter as a mere child
and as a woman, fresh upon me, it is natural that I
should linger on my way to the close of this brief record, avoiding its end. But, even as the close came
upon her, so must it come here.

Always impelled by an intense conviction that her
life must not be dreamed away, and that her indulgence
in her favourite pursuits must be balanced by action in
the real world around her, she was indefatigable in her
endeavours to do some good. Naturally enthusiastic,
and conscientiously impressed with a deep sense of her
Christian duty to her neighbour, she devoted herself to
a variety of benevolent objects. Now, it was the visi-

tation of the sick, that had possession of her; now, it was the sheltering of the houseless; now, it was the elementary teaching of the densely ignorant; now, it was the raising up of those who had wandered and got trodden under foot; now, it was the wider employment of her own sex in the general business of life; now, it was all these things at once. Perfectly unselfish, swift to sympathize and eager to relieve, she wrought at such designs with a flushed earnestness that disregarded season, weather, time of day or night, food, rest. Under such a hurry of the spirits, and such incessant occupation, the strongest constitution will commonly go down. Hers, neither of the strongest nor the weakest, yielded to the burden, and began to sink.

To have saved her life, then, by taking action on the warning that shone in her eyes and sounded in her voice, would have been impossible, without changing her nature. As long as the power of moving about in the old way was left to her, she must exercise it, or be killed by the restraint. And so the time came when she could move about no longer, and took to her bed.

All the restlessness gone then, and all the sweet patience of her natural disposition purified by the resignation of her soul, she lay upon her bed through the whole round of changes of the seasons. She lay upon her bed through fifteen months. In all that time, her old cheerfulness never quitted her. In all that time, not an impatient or a querulous minute can be re-membered.

At length, at midnight on the second of February

1864, she turned down a leaf of a little book she was reading, and shut it up.

The ministering hand that had copied the verses into the tiny album was soon around her neck, and she quietly asked, as the clock was on the stroke of one :

" Do you think I am dying, mamma? "

" I think you are very, very ill to-night, my dear."

" Send for my sister.   My feet are so cold.   Lift me up ! "

Her sister entering as they raised her, she said : "It has come at last !"   And with a bright and happy smile, looked upward, and departed.

Well had she written :

> Why shouldst thou fear the beautiful angel, Death,
> Who waits thee at the portals of the skies,
> Ready to kiss away thy struggling breath,
> Ready with gentle hand to close thine eyes?
>
> Oh what were life, if life were all?   Thine eyes
> Are blinded by their tears, or thou wouldst see
> Thy treasures wait thee in the far-off skies,
> And Death, thy friend, will give them all to thee.

THE ANGEL'S STORY.

THROUGH the blue and frosty heavens,
  Christmas stars were shining bright;
Glistening lamps throughout the City
Almost matched their gleaming light;
While the winter snow was lying,
And the winter winds were sighing,
  Long ago, one Christmas night.

While, from every tower and steeple,
  Pealing bells were sounding clear,
(Never with such tones of gladness,
  Save when Christmas time is near,)
Many a one that night was merry
  Who had toiled through all the year.

That night saw old wrongs forgiven,
  Friends, long parted, reconciled;
Voices all unused to laughter,
  Mournful eyes that rarely smiled,
Trembling hearts that feared the morrow
  From their anxious thoughts beguiled.

209

B

Rich and poor felt love and blessing
  From the gracious season fall;
Joy and plenty in the cottage,
  Peace and feasting in the hall;
And the voices of the children
  Ringing clear above it all!

Yet one house was dim and darkened:
  Gloom, and sickness, and despair,
Dwelling in the gilded chambers,
  Creeping up the marble stair,
Even stilled the voice of mourning—
  For a child lay dying there.

Silken curtains fell around him,
  Velvet carpets hushed the tread,
Many costly toys were lying,
  All unheeded, by his bed;
And his tangled golden ringlets
  Were on downy pillows spread.

The skill of all that mighty City
  To save one little life was vain;
One little thread from being broken
One fatal word from being spoken;
  Nay, his very mother's pain,
And the mighty love within her,
  Could not give him health again.

So she knelt there still beside him,
  She alone with strength to smile,

Promising that he should suffer
　No more in a little while,
Murmuring tender song and story
　Weary hours to beguile.

Suddenly an unseen Presence
　Checked those constant moaning cries,
Stilled the little heart's quick fluttering,
　Raised those blue and wondering eyes,
Fixed on some mysterious vision,
　With a startled sweet surprise.

For a radiant angel hovered,
　Smiling, o'er the little bed;
White his raiment, from his shoulders
　Snowy dove-like pinions spread,
And a starlike light was shining
　In a Glory round his head.

While, with tender love, the angel,
　Leaning o'er the little nest,
In his arms the sick child folding,
　Laid him gently on his breast,
Sobs and wailings told the mother
　That her darling was at rest.

So the angel, slowly rising,
　Spread his wings; and, through the air,
Bore the child, and while he held him
　To his heart with loving care,

Placed a branch of crimson roses
　　Tenderly beside him there.

While the child, thus clinging, floated
　　Towards the mansions of the Blest,
Gazing from his shining guardian
　　To the flowers upon his breast,
Thus the angel spake, still smiling
　　On the little heavenly guest :

" Know, dear little one, that Heaven
　　Does no earthly thing disdain,
Man's poor joys find there an echo
　　Just as surely as his pain ;
Love, on earth so feebly striving,
　　Lives divine in Heaven again !

" Once in that great town below us,
　　In a poor and narrow street,
Dwelt a little sickly orphan ;
　　Gentle aid, or pity sweet,
Never in life's rugged pathway
　　Guided his poor tottering feet.

" All the striving anxious forethought
　　That should only come with age,
Weighed upon his baby spirit,
　　Showed him soon life's sternest page ;
Grim Want was his nurse, and Sorrow
　　Was his only heritage.

" All too weak for childish pastimes,
    Drearily the hours sped;
On his hands so small and trembling
    Leaning his poor aching head,
Or, through dark and painful hours,
    Lying sleepless on his bed.

" Dreaming strange and longing fancies
    Of cool forests far away;
And of rosy, happy children,
    Laughing merrily at play,
Coming home through green lanes, bearing
    Trailing boughs of blooming May.

" Scarce a glimpse of azure heaven
    Gleamed above that narrow street, ·
And the sultry air of Summer
    (That you call so warm and sweet)
Fevered the poor Orphan, dwelling
    In the crowded alley's heat.

" One bright day, with feeble footsteps
    Slowly forth he tried to crawl,
Through the crowded city's pathways,
    Till he reached a garden-wall;
Where 'mid princely halls and mansions
    Stood the lordliest of all.

" There were trees with giant branches,
    Velvet glades where shadows hide :

There were sparkling fountains glancing,
  Flowers, which in luxuriant pride
Even wafted breaths of perfume
  To the child who stood outside

" He against the gate of iron
  Pressed his wan and wistful face,
Gazing with an awe-struck pleasure
  At the glories of the place ;
Never had his brightest day-dream
  Shone with half such wondrous grace.

" You were playing in that garden,
  Throwing blossoms in the air,
Laughing when the petals floated
  Downwards on your golden hair ;
And the fond eyes watching o'er you,
And the splendour spread before you,
  Told a House's Hope was there.

" When your servants, tired of seeing
  Such a face of want and woe,
Turning to the ragged Orphan,
  Gave him coin, and bade him go,
Down his cheeks so thin and wasted,
  Bitter tears began to flow.

' But that look of childish sorrow
  On your tender child-heart fell,
And you plucked the reddest roses
  From the tree you loved so well,

Passed them through the stern cold grating,
  Gently bidding him ' Farewell !"

" Dazzled by the fragrant treasure
  And the gentle voice he heard,
In the poor forlorn boy's spirit,
  Joy, the sleeping Seraph, stirred ;
In his hand he took the flowers,
  In his heart the loving word.

" So he crept to his poor garret :
  Poor no more, but rich and bright,
For the holy dreams of childhood—
  Love, and Rest, and Hope, and Light—
Floated round the Orphan's pillow
  Through the starry summer night.

" Day dawned, yet the visions lasted ;
  All too weak to rise he lay ;
Did he dream that none spake harshly—
  All were strangely kind that day ?
Surely then his treasured roses
  Must have charmed all ills away.

" And he smiled, though they were fading ;
  One by one their leaves were shed ;
' Such bright things could never perish,
  They would bloom again,' he said.
When the next day's sun had risen
  Child and flowers both were dead.

" Know, dear little one ! our Father
    Will no gentle deed disdain ;
Love on the cold earth beginning
    Lives divine in Heaven again,
While the angel hearts that beat there
    Still all tender thoughts retain."

So the angel ceased, and gently
    O'er his little burthen leant ;
While the child gazed from the shining,
    Loving eyes that o'er him bent,
To the blooming roses by him,
    Wondering what that mystery meant.

Thus the radiant angel answered,
    And with tender meaning smiled :
" Ere your childlike, loving spirit,
    Sin and the hard world defiled,
God has given me leave to seek you—
    I was once that little child !"

*   *   *   *

In the churchyard of that city
    Rose a tomb of marble rare,
Decked, as soon as Spring awakened,
    With her buds and blossoms fair—
And a humble grave beside it—
    No one knew who rested there.

ECHOES.

STILL the angel stars are shining,
   Still the rippling waters flow,
But the angel-voice is silent
   That I heard so long ago.
Hark ! the echoes murmur low,
          Long ago !

Still the wood is dim and lonely,
   Still the plashing fountains play,
But the past and all its beauty,
   Whither has it fled away ?
Hark ! the mournful echoes say,
          Fled away !

Still the bird of night complaineth,
   (Now, indeed, her song is pain,)
Visions of my happy hours,
   Do I call and call in vain?
Hark ! the echoes cry again,
          All in vain !

Cease, oh echoes, mournful echoes !
   Once I loved your voices well ;
Now my heart is sick and weary—

Days of old, a long farewell !
Hark ! the echoes sad and dreary
    Cry farewell, farewell !

A FALSE GENIUS.

SEE a Spirit by thy side,
Purple-winged and eagle-eyed,
Looking like a Heavenly guide.

Though he seem so bright and fair,
Ere thou trust his proffered care,
Pause a little, and beware !

If he bid thee dwell apart,
Tending some ideal smart
In a sick and coward heart ;

In self-worship wrapped alone,
Dreaming thy poor griefs are grown
More than other men have known,

Dwelling in some cloudy sphere,
Though God's work is waiting here,
And God deigneth to be near ;

If his torch's crimson glare
Show thee evil everywhere,
Tainting all the wholesome air ;

While with strange distorted choice,
Still disdaining to rejoice,
Thou *wilt* hear a wailing voice;

If a simple, humble heart,
Seem to thee a meaner part,
Than thy noblest aim and art;

If he bid thee bow before
Crownèd Mind and nothing more,
The great idol men adore;

And with starry veil enfold
Sin, the trailing serpent old,
Till his scales shine out like gold;

Though his words seem true and wise,
Soul, I say to thee—Arise,
He is a Demon in disguise!

MY PICTURE.

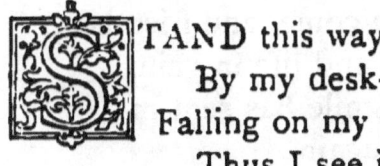'TAND this way—more near the window—
By my desk—you see the light
Falling on my picture better—
Thus I see it while I write!

Who the head may be I know not,
 But it has a student air;
With a look half sad, half stately,
 Grave sweet eyes and flowing hair.

Little care I who the painter,
 How obscure a name he bore;
Nor, when some have named Velasquez,
 Did I value it the more.

As it is, I would not give it
 For the rarest piece of art;
It has dwelt with me, and listened
 To the secrets of my heart.

Many a time, when to my garret,
 Weary, I returned at night,
It has seemed to look a welcome
 That has made my poor room bright.

Many a time, when ill and sleepless,
 I have watched the quivering gleam
Of my lamp upon that picture,
 Till it faded in my dream.

When dark days have come, and friendship
 Worthless seemed, and life in vain,
That bright friendly smile has sent me
 Boldly to my task again.

Sometimes when hard need has pressed me
   To bow down where I despise,
I have read stern words of counsel
   In those sad reproachful eyes.

Nothing that my brain imagined,
   Or my weary hand has wrought,
But it watched the dim Idea
   Spring forth into armèd Thought.

It has smiled on my successes,
   Raised me when my hopes were low,
And by turns has looked upon me
   With all the loving eyes I know.

Do you wonder that my picture
   Has become so like a friend?—
It has seen my life's beginnings,
   It shall stay and cheer the end!

JUDGE NOT.

JUDGE not; the workings of his brain
   And of his heart thou canst not see;
What looks to thy dim eyes a stain,
   In God's pure light may only be
A scar, brought from some well-won field,
Where thou wouldst only faint and yield.

The look, the air, that frets thy sight,
    May be a token, that below
The soul has closed in deadly fight
    With some infernal fiery foe,
Whose glance would scorch thy smiling grace,
And cast thee shuddering on thy face !

The fall thou darest to despise—
    May be the angel's slackened hand
Has suffered it, that he may rise
    And take a firmer, surer stand ;
Or, trusting less to earthly things,
May henceforth learn to use his wings.

And judge none lost ; but wait, and see,
    With hopeful pity, not disdain ;
The depth of the abyss may be
    The measure of the height of pain
And love and glory that may raise
    This soul to God in after days !

FRIEND SORROW.

DO not cheat thy Heart and tell her,
  "Grief will pass away,
  Hope for fairer times in future,
And forget to-day."—
Tell her, if you will, that sorrow
  Need not come in vain ;
Tell her that the lesson taught her
  Far outweighs the pain.

Cheat her not with the old comfort,
  "Soon she will forget"—
Bitter truth, alas—but matter
  Rather for regret ;
Bid her not "Seek other pleasures,
  Turn to other things :"—
Rather nurse her cagèd sorrow
  'Till the captive sings.

Rather bid her go forth bravely,
  And the stranger greet ;
Not as foe, with spear and buckler,
  But as dear friends meet ;
Bid her with a strong clasp hold her
By her dusky wings—
Listening for the murmured blessing
  Sorrow always brings.

ONE BY ONE.

ONE by one the sands are flowing,
   One by one the moments fall ;
   Some are coming, some are going ;
Do not strive to grasp them all.

One by one thy duties wait thee,
   Let thy whole strength go to each,
Let no future dreams elate thee,
   Learn thou first what these can teach.

One by one (bright gifts from Heaven)
   Joys are sent thee here below ;
Take them readily when given,
   Ready too to let them go.

One by one thy griefs shall meet thee,
   Do not fear an armèd band ;
One will fade as others greet thee ;
   Shadows passing through the land.

Do not look at life's long sorrow ;
   See how small each moment's pain ;
God will help thee for to-morrow,
   So each day begin again.

One by One.

Every hour that fleets so slowly
   Has its task to do or bear;
Luminous the crown, and holy,
   When each gem is set with care.

Do not linger with regretting,
   Or for passing hours despond;
Nor, the daily toil forgetting,
   Look too eagerly beyond.

Hours are golden links, God's token,
   Reaching Heaven; but one by one
Take them, lest the chain be broken
   Ere the pilgrimage be done.

TRUE HONOURS.

IS my darling tired already,
    Tired of her day of play?
    Draw your little stool beside me,
Smooth this tangled hair away.
Can she put the logs together,
   Till they make a cheerful blaze?
Shall her blind old Uncle tell her
   Something of his youthful days?

Hark! The wind among the cedars
   Waves their white arms to and fro;

I remember how I watched them
   Sixty Christmas Days ago:
Then I dreamt a glorious vision
   Of great deeds to crown each year—
Sixty Christmas Days have found me
   Useless, helpless, blind—and here!

Yes, I feel my darling stealing
   Warm soft fingers into mine—
Shall I tell her what I fancied
   In that strange old dream of mine?
I was kneeling by the window,
   Reading how a noble band,
With the red cross on their breast-plates,
   Went to gain the Holy Land.

While with eager eyes of wonder
   Over the dark page I bent,
Slowly twilight shadows gathered
   Till the letters came and went;
Slowly, till the night was round me;
   Then my heart beat loud and fast,
For I felt before I saw it
   That a spirit near me passed.

Then I raised my eyes, and shining
   Where the moon's first ray was bright
Stood a wingèd Angel-warrior
   Clothed and panoplied in light:
So, with Heaven's love upon him,
   Stern in calm and resolute will,

Looked St. Michael—does the picture
   Hang in the old cloister still?

Threefold were the dreams of honour
   That absorbed my heart and brain;
Threefold crowns the Angel promised,
   Each one to be bought by pain:
While he spoke, a threefold blessing
   Fell upon my soul like rain.
HELPER OF THE POOR AND SUFFERING;
   VICTOR IN A GLORIOUS STRIFE;
SINGER OF A NOBLE POEM:
   Such the honours of my life.

Ah, that dream! Long years that gave me
   Joy and grief as real things
Never touched the tender memory
   Sweet and solemn that it brings—
Never quite effaced the feeling
   Of those white and shadowing wings.

Do those blue eyes open wider?
   Does my faith too foolish seem?
Yes, my darling, years have taught me
   It was nothing but a dream.
Soon, too soon, the bitter knowledge
   Of a fearful trial rose,
Rose to crush my heart, and sternly
   Bade my young ambition close.

More and more my eyes were clouded,
   Till at last God's glorious light

Passed away from me for ever,
  And I lived and live in night.
Dear, I will not dim your pleasure,
  Christmas should be only gay—
In my night the stars have risen,
  And I wait the dawn of day.

Spite of all I could be happy ;
  For my brothers' tender care
In their boyish pastimes ever
  Made me take, or feel a share.
Philip, even then so thoughtful,
  Max so noble, brave and tall,
And your father, little Godfrey,
  The most loving of them all.

Philip reasoned down my sorrow,
  Max would laugh my gloom away,
Godfrey's little arms put round me,
  Helped me through my dreariest day ;
While the promise of my Angel,
  Like a star, now bright, now pale,
Hung in blackest night above me,
  And I felt it could not fail.

Years passed on, my brothers left me,
  Each went out to take his share
In the struggle of life ; my portion
  Was a humble one—to bear.
Here I dwelt, and learnt to wander
  Through the woods and fields alone,

Every cottage in the village
    Had a corner called my own.

Old and young, all brought their troubles,
    Great or small, for me to hear ;
I have often blessed my sorrow
    That drew others' grief so near.
Ah, the people needed helping—
    Needed love—(for Love and Heaven
Are the only gifts not bartered,
    They alone are freely given)—

And I gave it.   Philip's bounty,
    (We were orphans, dear,) made toil
Prosper, and want never fastened
    On the tenants of the soil.
Philip's name (Oh, how I gloried,
    He so young, to see it rise !)
Soon grew noted among statesmen
    As a patriot true and wise.

And his people all felt honoured
    To be ruled by such a name ;
I was proud too that they loved me;
    Through their pride in him it came.
He had gained what I had longed for,
    I meanwhile grew glad and gay,
'Mid his people, to be serving
    Him and them, in some poor way.

How his noble earnest speeches,
　　With untiring fervour came ;
HELPER OF THE POOR AND SUFFERING ;
　　Truly he deserved the name !
Had my Angel's promise failed me ?
　　Had that word of hope grown dim ?
Why, my Philip had fulfilled it,
　　And I loved it best in him !

Max meanwhile—ah, you, my darling,
　　Can his loving words recall—
'Mid the bravest and the noblest,
　　Braver, nobler, than them all.
How I loved him ! how my heart thrilled
　　When his sword clanked by his side,
When I touched his gold embroidery,
　　Almost *saw* him in his pride !

So we parted ; he all eager
　　To uphold the name he bore,
Leaving in my charge—he loved me—
　　Some one whom he loved still more :
I must tend this gentle flower,
　　I must speak to her of him,
For he feared—Love still is fearful—
　　That his memory might grow dim.

I must guard her from all sorrow,
　　I must play a brother's part,
Shield all grief and trial from her,
　　If it need be, with my heart.

Years passed, and his name grew famous;
   We were proud, both she and I ;
And we lived upon his letters,
   While the slow days fleeted by.

Then at last—you know the story,
   How a fearful rumour spread,
Till all hope had slowly faded,
   And we heard that he was dead.
Dead ! Oh, those were bitter hours ;
   Yet within my soul there dwelt
A warning, and while others mourned him,
   Something like a hope I felt.

His was no weak life as mine was,
   But a life, so full and strong—
No, I could not think he perished
   Nameless, 'mid a conquered throng.
How she drooped ! Years passed ; no tidings
   Came, and yet that little flame
Of strange hope within my spirit
   Still burnt on, and lived the same.

Ah ! my child, our hearts will fail us,
   When to us they strongest seem
I can look back on those hours
   As a fearful, evil dream.
She had long despaired ; what wonder
   That her heart had turned to mine ?
Earthly loves are deep and tender,
   Not eternal and divine !

Can I say how bright a future
    Rose before my soul that day?
Oh, so strange, so sweet, so tender—
    And I had to turn away.
Hard and terrible the struggle,
    For the pain not mine alone;
I called back my Brother's spirit,
    And I bade him claim his own.

Told her—now I dared to do it—
    That I felt the day would rise
When he would return to gladden
    My weak heart and her bright eyes.
And I pleaded—pleaded sternly—
    In his name, and for his sake:
Now, I can speak calmly of it,
    Then, I thought my heart would break.

Soon—ah, Love had not deceived me,
    (Love's true instincts never err,)
Wounded, weak, escaped from prison,
    He returned to me; to her.
I could thank God that bright morning,
    When I felt my Brother's gaze,
That my heart was true and loyal,
    As in our old boyish days.

Bought by wounds and deeds of daring,
    Honours he had brought away;
Glory crowned his name—my Brother's;
    Mine too!—we were one that day.

True Honours.

Since the crown on him had fallen,
  "VICTOR IN A NOBLE STRIFE,"
I could live and die contented
  With my poor ignoble life.

Well, my darling, almost weary
  Of my story? Wait awhile;
For the rest is only joyful;
  I can tell it with a smile.
One bright promise still was left me,
  Wound so close about my soul,
That, as one by one had failed me,
  This dream now absorbed the whole.

"SINGER OF A NOBLE POEM,"—
  Ah, my darling, few and rare
Burn the glorious names of Poets,
  Like stars in the purple air.
That too, and I glory in it,
  That great gift my Godfrey won;
I have my dear share of honour,
  Gained by that belovèd one.

One day shall my darling read it;
  Now she cannot understand
All the noble thoughts, that lighten
  Through the genius of the land.
I am proud to be his brother,
  Proud to think that hope was true;
Though I longed and strove so vainly
  What I failed in, he could do.

I was long before I knew it,
  Longer ere I felt it so ;
Then I strung my rhymes together
  Only for the poor and low.
And, it pleases me to know it,
  (For I love them well indeed,)
They care for my humble verses,
  Fitted for their humble need.

And, it cheers my heart to hear it,
  Where the far-off settlers roam,
My poor words are sung and cherished,
  Just because they speak of Home.
And the little children sing them,
  (That, I think, has pleased me best,)
Often, too, the dying love them,
  For they tell of Heaven and rest.

So my last vain dream has faded :
  (Such as I to think of fame !)
Yet I will not say it failed me,
  For it crowned my Godfrey's name
No ; my Angel did not cheat me,
  For my long life *has* been blest ;
He did give me Love and Sorrow,
  He will bring me Light and Rest.

A WOMAN'S QUESTION.

BEFORE I trust my Fate to thee,
    Or place my hand in thine,
    Before I let thy Future give
Colour and form to mine,
Before I peril all for thee, question thy soul to-night
    for me.

I break all slighter bonds, nor feel
    A shadow of regret :
Is there one link within the Past,
    That holds thy spirit yet ?
Or is thy Faith as clear and free as that which I can
    pledge to thee ?

Does there within thy dimmest dreams
    A possible future shine,
Wherein thy life could henceforth breathe,
    Untouched, unshared by mine ?
If so, at any pain or cost, oh, tell me before all is lost.

Look deeper still. If thou canst feel
    Within thy inmost soul,
That thou hast kept a portion back,
    While I have staked the whole ;
Let no false pity spare the blow, but in true mercy tell
    me so.

Is there within thy heart a need
  That mine cannot fulfil?
One chord that any other hand
  Could better wake or still?
Speak now—lest at some future day my whole life
    wither and decay.

Lives there within thy nature hid
  The demon-spirit Change,
Shedding a passing glory still
  On all things new and strange?—
It may not be thy fault alone—but shield my heart
    against thy own.

Couldst thou withdraw thy hand one day
  And answer to my claim,
That Fate, and that to-day's mistake,
  Not thou—had been to blame?
Some soothe their conscience thus: but thou, wilt surely
    warn and save me now.

Nay, answer *not*—I dare not hear,
  The words would come too late;
Yet I would spare thee all remorse,
  So, comfort thee, my Fate—
Whatever on my heart may fall—remember. I *would*
    risk it all!

THE THREE RULERS.

 SAW a Ruler take his stand
    And trample on a mighty land;
The People crouched before his beck,
His iron heel was on their neck,
His name shone bright through blood and pain,
His sword flashed back their praise again.

I saw another Ruler rise—
His words were noble, good, and wise;
With the calm sceptre of his pen
He ruled the minds and thoughts of men:
Some scoffed, some praised—while many heard,
Only a few obeyed his word.

Another Ruler then I saw—
Love and sweet Pity were his law:
The greatest and the least had part
(Yet most the unhappy) in his heart—
The People, in a mighty band,
Rose up, and drove him from the land!

A DEAD PAST.

SPARE her at least : look, you have taken from me
The Present, and I murmur not, nor moan ;
The Future too, with all her glorious promise ;
But do not leave me utterly alone.

Spare me the Past—for, see, she cannot harm you,
She lies so white and cold, wrapped in her shroud ;
All, all my own ; and, trust me, I will hide her
Within my soul, nor speak to her aloud.

I folded her soft hands upon her bosom,
And strewed my flowers upon her—*they* still live—
Sometimes I like to kiss her closed white eyelids,
And think of all the joy she used to give.

Cruel indeed it were to take her from me ;
She sleeps, she will not wake—no fear—again :
And so I laid her, such a gentle burthen,
Quietly on my heart to still its pain.

I do not think that any smiling Present,
Any vague Future, spite of all her charms,
Conld ever rival her.   You know you laid her,
Long years ago, then living, in my arms.

Leave her at least—while my tears fall upon her,
I dream she smiles, just as she did of yore;
As dear as ever to me—nay, it may be,
Even dearer still—since I have nothing more.

A DOUBTING HEART.

WHERE are the swallows fled?
  Frozen and dead,
  Perchance upon some bleak and stormy
shore.
  Oh doubting heart!
  Far over purple seas,
  They wait, in sunny ease,
  The balmy southern breeze,
To bring them to their northern homes once more.

Why must the flowers die?
  Prisoned they lie
In the cold tomb, heedless of tears or rain.
  Oh doubting heart!
  They only sleep below
  The soft white ermine snow,
  While winter winds shall blow,
To breathe and smile upon you soon again.

The sun has hid its rays
  These many days;

Will dreary hours never leave the earth?
  Oh doubting heart !
  The stormy clouds on high
  Veil the same sunny sky,
  That soon (for spring is nigh)
Shall wake the summer into golden mirth.

Fair hope is dead, and light
  Is quenched in night.
What sound can break the silence of despair?
  Oh doubting heart !
  Thy sky is overcast,
  Yet stars shall rise at last,
  Brighter for darkness past,
And angels' silver voices stir the air.

A STUDENT.

OVER an ancient scroll I bent,
 Steeping my soul in wise content,
 Nor paused a moment, save to chide
A low voice whispering at my side.

I wove beneath the stars' pale shrine
A dream, half human, half divine;
And shook off (not to break the charm)
A little hand laid on my arm.

I read; until my heart would glow
With the great deeds of long ago;
Nor heard, while with those mighty dead,
Pass to and fro a faltering tread.

On the old theme I pondered long—
The struggle between right and wrong;
I could not check such visions high,
To soothe a little quivering sigh.

I tried to solve the problem—Life;
Dreaming of that mysterious strife,
How could I leave such reasonings wise,
To answer two blue pleading eyes?

I strove how best to give, and when,
My blood to save my fellow-men—
How could I turn aside, to look
At snowdrops laid upon my book?

Now Time has fled—the world is strange,
Something there is of pain and change;
My books lie closed upon the shelf;
I miss the old heart in myself.

I miss the sunbeams in my room —
It was not always wrapped in gloom:
I miss my dreams—they fade so fast,
Or flit into some trivial past.

The great stream of the world goes by;
None care, or heed, or question, why
I, the lone student, cannot raise
My voice or hand as in old days.

No echo seems to wake again
My heart to anything but pain,
Save when a dream of twilight brings
The fluttering of an angel's wings!

A KNIGHT ERRANT.

THOUGH he lived and died among us,
 Yet his name may be enrolled
With the knights whose deeds of daring
 Ancient chronicles have told.

Still a stripling, he encountered
 Poverty, and struggled long,
Gathering force from every effort,
 Till he knew his arm was strong.

Then his heart and life he offered
 To his radiant mistress—Truth;
Never thought, or dream, or faltering,
 Marred the promise of his youth.

So he rode forth to defend her,
    And her peerless worth proclaim ;
Challenging each recreant doubter
    Who aspersed her spotless name.

First upon his path stood Ignorance,
    Hideous in his brutal might ;
Hard the blows and long the battle
    Ere the monster took to flight.

Then, with light and fearless spirit,
    Prejudice he dared to brave ;
Hunting back the lying craven
    To her black sulphureous cave.

Followed by his servile minions,
    Custom, the old Giant, rose ;
Yet he, too, at last was conquered
    By the good Knight's weighty blows.

Then he turned, and, flushed with victory,
    Struck upon the brazen shield
Of the world's great king, Opinion,
    And defied him to the field.

Once again he rose a conqueror,
    And, though wounded in the fight,
With a dying smile of triumph
    Saw that Truth had gained her right.

On his failing ear re-echoing
    Came the shouting round her throne;
Little cared he that no future
    With her name would link his own.

Spent with many a hard-fought battle,
    Slowly ebbed his life away,
And the crowd that flocked to greet her
    Trampled on him where he lay.

Gathering all his strength, he saw her
    Crowned and reigning in her pride:
Looked his last upon her beauty,
    Raised his eyes to God, and died.

LINGER, OH, GENTLE TIME.

LINGER, oh, gentle Time,
    Linger, oh, radiant grace of bright To-day!
      Let not the hours' chime
        Call thee away,
But linger near me still with fond delay.

      Linger, for thou art mine!
What dearer treasures can the future hold?
      What sweeter flowers than thine
        Can she unfold?
What secrets tell my heart thou hast not told?

Oh, linger in thy flight !
For shadows gather round, and should we part,
 A dreary starless night
  May fill my heart,—
Then pause and linger yet ere thou depart.

 Linger, I ask no more,—
Thou art enough for ever—thou alone ;
 What future can restore,
  When thou art flown,
All that I hold from thee and call my own ?

HOMEWARD BOUND.

I HAVE seen a fiercer tempest,
 Known a louder whirlwind blow ;
I was wrecked off red Algiers,
 Six-and-thirty years ago.
Young I was, and yet old seamen
 Were not strong or calm as I ;
While life held such treasures for me,
 I felt sure I could not die.

Life I struggled for—and saved it ;
 Life alone—and nothing more ;
Bruised, half dead, alone and helpless,
 I was cast upon the shore.

I feared the piti ess rocks of Ocean
  So the great sea rose—and then
Cast me from her friendly bosom,
  On the pitiless hearts of men.

Gaunt and dreary ran the mountains,
  With black gorges, up the land;
Up to where the lonely Desert
  Spreads her burning, dreary sand:
In the gorges of the mountains,
  On the plain beside the sea,
Dwelt my stern and cruel masters,
  The black Moors of Barbary.

Ten long years I toiled among them,
  Hopeless—as I used to say;
Now I know Hope burnt within me
  Fiercer, stronger, day by day:
Those dim years of toil and sorrow
  Like one long dark dream appear;
One long day of weary waiting—
  Then each day was like a year.

How I cursed the land—my prison;
  How I cursed the serpent sea—
And the Demon Fate that showered
  All her curses upon me;
I was mad, I think—God pardon
  Words so terrible and wild—
This voyage would have been my last one,
  For I left a wife and child.

Never did one tender vision
   Fade away before my sight,
Never once through all my slavery,
   Burning day or dreary night;
In my soul it lived, and kept me,
   Now I feel, from black despair,
And my heart was not quite broken,
   While they lived and blest me there.

When at night my task was over,
   I would hasten to the shore;
(All was strange and foreign inland,
   Nothing I had known before;)
Strange looked the bleak mountain passes,
   Strange the red glare and black shade,
And the Oleanders, waving
   To the sound the fountains made.

Then I gazed at the great Ocean,
   Till she grew a friend again;
And because she knew old England,
   I forgave her all my pain:
So the blue still sky above me,
   With its white clouds' fleecy fold,
And the glimmering stars, (though brighter,)
   Looked like home and days of old.

And a calm would fall upon me,
   Worn perhaps with work and pain,
The wild hungry longing left me,
   And I was myself again:

Looking at the silver waters,
  Looking up at the far sky,
Dreams of home and all I left there
  Floated sorrowfully by.

A fair face, but pale with sorrow,
  With blue eyes, brimful of tears,
And the little red mouth, quivering
  With a smile, to hide its fears ;
Holding out her baby towards me,
  From the sky she looked on me ;
So it was that last I saw her,
  As the ship put out to sea.

Sometimes, (and a pang would seize me
  That the years were floating on,)
I would strive to paint her, altered,
  And the little baby gone :
She no longer young and girlish,
  The child, standing by her knee,
And her face, more pale and saddened
  With the weariness for me.

Then I saw, as night grew darker,
  How she taught my child to pray,
Holding its small hands together,
  For its father, far away ;
And I felt her sorrow, weighing
  Heavier on me than my own ;
Pitying her blighted spring-time,
  And her joy so early flown.

Till upon my hands (now hardened
  With the rough, harsh toil of years)
Bitter drops of anguish falling,
  Woke me from my dream, to tears ;
Woke me as a slave, an outcast,
  Leagues from home, across the deep ;
So—though you may call it childish—
  So I sobbed myself to sleep.

Well, the years sped on—my Sorrow,
  Calmer, and yet stronger grown,
Was my shield against all suffering,
  Poorer, meaner, than her own.
Thus my cruel master's harshness
  Fell upon me all in vain,
Yet the tale of what we suffered
  Echoed back from main to main.

You have heard in a far country
  Of a self-devoted band,
Vowed to rescue Christian captives
  Pining in a foreign land.
And these gentle-hearted strangers
  Year by year go forth from Rome,
In their hands the hard-earned ransom,
  To restore some exiles home.

I was freed : they broke the tidings
  Gently to me : but indeed
Hour by hour sped on, I knew not
  What the words meant—I was freed !

Better so, perhaps ; while sorrow
  (More akin to earthly things)
Only strains the sad heart's fibres—
  Joy, bright stranger, breaks the strings.

Yet at last it rushed upon me,
  And my heart beat full and fast ;
What were now my years of waiting,
  What was all the dreary past?
Nothing—to the impatient throbbing
  I must bear across the sea :
Nothing—to the eternal hours
  Still between my home and me !

How the voyage passed, I know not ;
  Strange it was once more to stand
With my countrymen around me,
  And to clasp an English hand.
But, through all, my heart was dreaming
  Of the first words I should hear,
In the gentle voice that echoed,
  Fresh as ever, on my ear.

Should I see her start of wonder,
  And the sudden truth arise,
Flushing all her face and lightening
  The dimmed splendour of her eyes ?
Oh ! to watch the fear and doubting
  Stir the silent depths of pain,
And the rush of joy—then melting
  Into perfect peace again.

And the child !—but why remember
  Foolish fancies that I thought ?
Every tree and every hedge-row
  From the well-known past I brought :
I would picture my dear cottage,
  See the crackling wood-fire burn,
And the two beside it seated,
  Watching, waiting, my return.

So, at last we reached the harbour.
  I remember nothing more
Till I stood, my sick heart throbbing,
  With my hand upon the door.
There I paused—I heard her speaking;
  Low, soft, murmuring words she said;
Then I first knew the dumb terror
  I had had, lest she were dead.

It was evening in late autumn,
  And the gusty wind blew chill;
Autumn leaves were falling round me,
  And the red sun lit the hill.
Six-and-twenty years are vanished
  Since then—I am old and grey—
But I never told to mortal
  What I saw, until this day.

She was seated by the fire,
  In her arms she held a child,
Whispering baby-words caressing,
  And then, looking up, she smiled :

Smiled on him who stood beside her—
   Oh ! the bitter truth was told,
In her look of trusting fondness—
   I had seen the look of old !

But she rose and turned towards me
   (Cold and dumb I waited there)
With a shriek of fear and terror,
   And a white face of despair.
He had been an ancient comrade—
   Not a single word we said,
While we gazed upon each other,
   He the living : I the dead !

I drew nearer, nearer to her,
   And I took her trembling hand,
Looking on her white face, looking
   That her heart might understand
All the love and all the pity
   That my lips refused to say—
I thank God no thought save sorrow
   Rose in our crushed hearts that day,

Bitter tears that desolate moment,
   Bitter, bitter tears we wept,
We three broken hearts together,
   While the baby smiled and slept.
Tears alone—no words were spoken,
   Till he—till her husband said
That my boy, (I had forgotten
   The poor child,) that he was dead.

Then at last I rose, and, turning,
  Wrung his hand, but made no sign;
And I stooped and kissed her forehead
  Once more, as if she were mine.
Nothing of farewell I uttered,
  Save in broken words to pray
That God would ever guard and bless her—
  Then in silence passed away.

Over the great restless ocean
  Six-and-twenty years I roam;
All my comrades, old and weary,
  Have gone back to die at home.—
Home! yes, I shall reach a haven,
  I, too, shall reach home and rest;
I shall find her waiting for me
  With our baby on her breast.

LIFE AND DEATH.

"WHAT is Life, Father?"
            "A Battle, my child,
  Where the strongest lance may fail,
Where the wariest eyes may be beguiled,
  And the stoutest heart may quail.
Where the foes are gathered on every hand
  And rest not day or night,

And the feeble little ones must stand
    In the thickest of the fight."

" What is Death, Father ? "

                      " The rest, my child.
    When the strife and the toil are o'er ;
The Angel of God, who, calm and mild,
    Says we need fight no more ;
Who, driving away the demon band,
    Bids the din of the battle cease ;
Takes banner and spear from our failing hand,
    And proclaims an eternal Peace."

" Let me die, Father ! I tremble, and fear
    To yield in that terrible strife ! "

" The crown must be won for Heaven, dear,
    In the battle-field of life :
My child, though thy foes are strong and tried,
    He loveth the weak and small ;
The Angels of Heaven are on thy side,
    And God is over all ! "

NOW.

RISE! for the day is passing,
  And you lie dreaming on;
  The others have buckled their armour,
  And forth to the fight are gone:
A place in the ranks awaits you,
  Each man has some part to play;
The Past and the Future are nothing,
  In the face of the stern To-day.

Rise from your dreams of the Future—
  Of gaining some hard-fought field;
Of storming some airy fortress,
  Or bidding some giant yield;
Your future has deeds of glory,
  Of honour (God grant it may!)
But your arm will never be stronger,
  Or the need so great as To-day.

Rise! if the Past detains you,
  Her sunshine and storms forget;
No chains so unworthy to hold you
  As those of a vain regret:
Sad or bright, she is lifeless ever,
  Cast her phantom arms away,

Nor look back, save to learn the lesson
    Of a nobler strife To-day.

Rise ! for the day is passing :
    The sound that you scarcely hear
Is the enemy marching to battle—
    Arise ! for the foe is here !
Stay not to sharpen your weapons,
    Or the hour will strike at last,
When, from dreams of a coming battle,
    You may wake to find it past!

CLEANSING FIRES.

LET thy gold be cast in the furnace,
    Thy red gold, precious and bright,
Do not fear the hungry fire,
    With its caverns of burning light :
And thy gold shall return more precious,
    Free from every spot and stain ;
For gold must be tried by fire,
    As a heart must be tried by pain !

In the cruel fire of Sorrow
    Cast thy heart, do not faint or wail ;
Let thy hand be firm and steady,
    Do not let thy spirit quail :

But wait till the trial is over,
  And take thy heart again;
For as gold is tried by fire,
  So a heart must be tried by pain !

I shall know by the gleam and glitter
  Of the golden chain you wear,
By your heart's calm strength in loving,
  Of the fire they have had to bear.
Beat on, true heart, for ever;
  Shine bright, strong golden chain ;
And bless the cleansing fire,
  And the furnace of living pain !

THE VOICE OF THE WIND.

LET us throw more logs on the fire !
    We have need of a cheerful light,
    And close round the hearth to gather,
  For the wind has risen to-night.
With the mournful sound of its wailing
  It has checked the children's glee,
And it calls with a louder clamour
  Than the clamour of the sea.
        Hark to the voice of the wind !

Let us listen to what it is saying,
  Let us hearken to where it has been ;

E

For it tells, in its terrible crying,
  The fearful sights it has seen.
It clatters loud at the casements,
  Round the house it hurries on,
And shrieks with redoubled fury,
  When we say " The blast is gone !"
        Hark to the voice of the wind !

It has been on the field of battle,
  Where the dying and wounded lie :
And it brings the last groan they uttered
  And the ravenous vulture's cry.
It has been where the icebergs were meeting,
  And closed with a fearful crash ;
On shores where no foot has wandered,
  It has heard the waters dash.
        Hark to the voice of the wind !

It has been on the desolate ocean,
  When the lightning struck the mast ;
It has heard the cry of the drowning,
  Who sank as it hurried past ;
The words of despair and anguish,
  'That were heard by no living ear ;
The gun that no signal answered :
  It brings them all to us here.
        Hark to the voice of the wind !

It has been on the lonely moorland,
  Where the treacherous snow-drift lies,

The Voice of the Wind.

Where the traveller, spent and weary,
  Gasped fainter and fainter cries;
It has heard the bay of the bloodhounds,
  On the track of the hunted slave,
The lash and the curse of the master,
  And the groan that the captive gave.
        Hark to the voice of the wind !

It has swept through the gloomy forest,
  Where the sledge was urged to its speed,
Where the howling wolves were rushing
  On the track of the panting steed.
Where the pool was black and lonely,
  It caught up a splash and a cry—
Only the bleak sky heard it,
  And the wind as it hurried by.
        Hark to the voice of the wind !

Then throw more logs on the fire,
  Since the air is bleak and cold,
And the children are drawing nigher,
  For the tales that the wind has told.
So closer and closer gather
  Round the red and crackling light ;
And rejoice (while the wind is blowing)
  We are safe and warm to-night.
        Hark to the voice of the wind !

TREASURES.

ET me count my treasures
　　All my soul holds dear,
　　Given me by dark spirits
Whom I used to fear.

Through long days of anguish,
　　And sad nights, did Pain
Forge my shield, Endurance,
　　Bright and free from stain !

Doubt, in misty caverns,
　　'Mid dark horrors sought,
Till my peerless jewel,
　　Faith to me she brought

Sorrow, that I wearied
　　Should remain so long,
Wreathed my starry glory,
　　The bright Crown of Song

Strife, that racked my spirit
　　Without hope or rest,
Left the blooming flower,
　　Patience, on my breast.

Suffering, that I dreaded,
    Ignorant of her charms,
Laid the fair child, Pity,
    Smiling, in my arms.

So I count my treasures,
    Stored in days long past—
And I thank the givers,
    Whom I know at last !

SHINING STARS.

HINE, ye stars of heaven,
    On a world of pain !
    See old Time destroying
All our hoarded gain ;
All our sweetest flowers,
    Every stately shrine,
All our hard-earned glory.
    Every dream divine !

Shine, ye stars of heaven,
    On the rolling years !
See how Time, consoling,
    Dries the saddest tears,

Bids the darkest storm-clouds
   Pass in gentle rain ;
While upspring in glory,
   Flowers and dreams again !

Shine, ye stars of heaven,
   On a world of fear !
See how Time, avenging,
   Bringeth judgment here ;
Weaving ill-won honours
   To a fiery crown ;
Bidding hard hearts perish ;
   Casting proud hearts down.

Shine, ye stars of heaven,
   On the hours' slow flight !
See how Time, rewarding,
   Gilds good deeds with light ;
Pays with kingly measure ;
   Brings earth's dearest prize ;
Or, crowned with rays diviner,
   Bids the end arise !

WAITING.

WHEREFORE dwell so sad and lonely,
  By the desolate sea-shore,
  With the melancholy surges
Beating at your cottage door?

"You shall dwell beside the castle
  Shadowed by our ancient trees;
And your life shall pass on gently,
  Cared for, and in rest and ease."

"Lady, one who loved me dearly
  Sailed for distant lands away;
And I wait here his returning
  Hopefully from day to day.

"To my door I bring my spinning,
  Watching every ship I see;
Waiting, hoping, till the sunset
  Fades into the western sea.

"After sunset, at my casement,
  Still I place a signal light;
He will see its well-known shining
  Should his ship return at night.

" Lady, see your infant smiling,
  With its flaxen curling hair—
I remember when your mother
  Was a baby just as fair.

" I was watching then, and hoping :
  Years have brought great change to all;
To my neighbours in their cottage,
  To you nobles at the hall.

" Not to me—for I am waiting,
  And the years have fled so fast,
I must look at you to tell me
  That a weary time has past !

" When I hear a footstep coming
  On the shingle—years have fled—
Yet amid a thousand others,
  I shall know his quick, light tread.

When I hear (to-night it may be)
  Some one pausing at my door,
I shall know the gay soft accents,
  Heard and welcomed oft before !

" So each day i am more hopeful,
  He may come before the night :
Every sunset I feel surer
  He must come ere morning light.

" Then I thank you, noble lady,
But I cannot do your will :
Where he left me, he must find me,
Waiting, watching, hoping, still !"

THE CRADLE SONG OF THE POOR.

HUSH ! I cannot bear to see thee
    Stretch thy tiny hands in vain ;
Dear, I have no bread to give thee,
    Nothing, child, to ease thy pain !
When God sent thee first to bless me,
    Proud, and thankful too, was I ;
Now, my darling, I, thy mother,
    Almost long to see thee die.
       Sleep, my darling, thou art weary;
       God is good, but life is dreary.

I have watched thy beauty fading,
    And thy strength sink day by day;
Soon, I know, will Want and Fever
    Take thy little life away.
Famine makes thy father reckless,
    Hope has left both him and me ;
We could suffer all, my baby,
    Had we but a crust for thee.
       Sleep, my darling, thou art weary ;
       God is good, but life is dreary.

Better thou shouldst perish early,
 Starve so soon, my darling one,
Than in helpless sin and sorrow
 Vainly live, as I have done.
Better that thy angel spirit
 With my joy, my peace, were flown,
Than thy heart grew cold and careless,
 Reckless, hopeless, like my own.
  Sleep, my darling, thou art weary;
  God is good, but life is dreary.

I am wasted, dear, with hunger,
 And my brain is all opprest,
I have scarcely strength to press thee,
 Wan and feeble, to my breast.
Patience, baby, God will help us,
 Death will come to thee and me,
He will take us to his Heaven,
 Where no want or pain can be.
  Sleep, my darling, thou art weary;
  God is good, but life is dreary.

Such the plaint that, late and early,
 Did we listen, we might hear
Close beside us,—but the thunder
 Of a city dulls our ear.
Every heart, as God's bright Angel,
 Can bid one such sorrow cease;
God has glory when his children
 Bring his poor ones joy and peace!
  Listen, nearer while she sings
  Sounds the fluttering of wings!

BE STRONG.

BE strong to *hope*, oh Heart !
 Though day is bright,
The stars can only shine
 In the dark night.
Be strong, oh Heart of mine,
 Look towards the light !

Be strong to *bear*, oh Heart !
 Nothing is vain :
Strive not, for life is care,
 And God sends pain,
Heaven is above, and there
 Rest will remain !

Be strong to *love*, oh Heart !
 Love knows not wrong,
Didst thou love—creatures even,
 Life were not long ;
Didst thou love God in Heaven,
 Thou wouldst be strong !

GOD'S GIFTS.

OD gave a gift to Earth :—a child,
Weak, innocent, and undefiled,
Opened its ignorant eyes and smiled.

It lay so helpless, so forlorn,
Earth took it coldly and in scorn,
Cursing the day when it was born.

She gave it first a tarnished name,
For heritage, a tainted fame,
Then cradled it in want and shame.

All influence of Good or Right,
All ray of God's most holy light,
She curtained closely from its sight.

Then turned her heart, her eyes away,
Ready to look again, the day
Its little feet began to stray.

In dens of guilt the baby played,
Where sin, and sin alone, was made
The law that all around obeyed.

With ready and obedient care,
He learnt the tasks they taught him there;
Black sin for lesson—oaths for prayer.

Then Earth arose, and, in her might,
To vindicate her injured right,
Thrust him in deeper depths of night.

Branding him with a deeper brand
Of shame, he could not understand,
The felon outcast of the land.

God gave a gift to Earth :—a child,
Weak, innocent, and undefiled,
Opened its ignorant eyes and smiled.

And Earth received the gift, and cried
Her joy and triumph far and wide,
Till echo answered to her pride.

She blest the hour when first he came
To take the crown of pride and fame,
Wreathed through long ages for his name.

Then bent her utmost art and skill
To train the supple mind and will,
And guard it from a breath of ill.

She strewed his morning path with flowers,
And Love, in tender dropping showers,
Nourished the blue and dawning hours.

She shed, in rainbow hues of light,
A halo round the Good and Right,
To tempt and charm the baby's sight.

And every step, of work or play,
Was lit by some such dazzling ray,
Till morning brightened into day.

And then the World arose, and said—
Let added honours now be shed
On such a noble heart and head !

O World, both gifts were pure and bright,
Holy and sacred in God's sight :—
God will judge them and thee aright !

A TOMB IN GHENT.

 SMILING look she had, a figure slight,
With cheerful air, and step both quick and
         light;
A strange and foreign look the maiden bore,
That suited the quaint Belgian dress she wore;
Yet the blue fearless eyes in her fair face,
And her soft voice told her of English race;
And ever, as she flitted to and fro,
She sang, (or murmured, rather,) soft and low,
Snatches of song, as if she did not know
That she was singing, but the happy load
Of dream and thought thus from her heart o'erflowed:
And while on household cares she passed along,
The air would bear me fragments of her song;
Not such as village maidens sing, and few
The framers of her changing music knew;
Chants such as heaven and earth first heard of when
The master Palestrina held the pen.
But I with awe had often turned the page,
Yellow with time, and half defaced by age,
And listened, with an ear not quite unskilled,
While heart and soul to the grand echo thrilled;
And much I marvelled, as her cadence fell
From the Laudate, that I knew so well,

Into Scarlatti's minor fugue, how she
Had learned such deep and solemn harmony.
But what she told I set in rhyme, as meet
To chronicle the influence, dim and sweet,
'Neath which her young and innocent life had grown :
Would that my words were simple as her own.

Many years since, an English workman went
Over the seas, to seek a home in Ghent,
Where English skill was prized ; nor toiled in vain ;
Small, yet enough, his hard-earned daily gain.
He dwelt alone—in sorrow, or in pride,
He mixed not with the workers by his side ;
He seemed to care but for one present joy—
To tend, to watch, to teach his sickly boy.
Severe to all beside, yet for the child
He softened his rough speech to soothings mild ;
For him he smiled, with him each day he walked
Through the dark gloomy streets ; to him he talked
Of home, of England, and strange stories told
Of English heroes in the days of old ;
And, (when the sunset gilded roof and spire,)
The marvellous tale which never seemed to tire :
How the gilt dragon, glaring fiercely down
From the great belfry, watching all the town,
Was brought, a trophy of the wars divine,
By a Crusader from far Palestine,
And given to Bruges ; and how Ghent arose,
And how they struggled long as deadly foes,
Till Ghent, one night, by a brave soldier's skill,

Stole the great dragon ; and she keeps it still.
One day the dragon—so 'tis said—will rise,
Spread his bright wings, and glitter in the skies,
And over desert lands and azure seas,
Will seek his home 'mid palm and cedar trees.
So, as he passed the belfry every day,
The boy would look if it were flown away ;
Each day surprised to find it watching there,
Above him, as he crossed the ancient square,
To seek the great cathedral, that had grown
A home for him—mysterious and his own.

Dim with dark shadows of the ages past,
St. Bavon stands, solemn and rich and vast ;
The slender pillars, in long vistas spread,
Like forest arches meet and close o'erhead ;
So high that, like a weak and doubting prayer,
Ere it can float to the carved angels there,
The silver clouded incense faints in air :
Only the organ's voice, with peal on peal,
Can mount to where those far-off angels kneel.
Here the pale boy, beneath a low side-arch,
Would listen to its solemn chant or march ;
Folding his little hands, his simple prayer
Melted in childish dreams, and both in air :
While the great organ over all would roll,
Speaking strange secrets to his innocent soul,
Bearing on eagle-wings the great desire
Of all the kneeling throng, and piercing higher
Than aught but love and prayer can reach, until

F

Only the silence seemed to listen still ;
Or gathering like a sea still more and more,
Break in melodious waves at heaven's door,
And then fall, slow and soft, in tender rain,
Upon the pleading longing hearts again.

Then he would watch the rosy sunlight glow,
That crept along the marble floor below,
Passing, as life does, with the passing hours,
Now by a shrine all rich with gems and flowers,
Now on the brazen letters of a tomb,
Then, leaving it again to shade and gloom,
And creeping on, to show, distinct and quaint,
The kneeling figure of some marble saint :
Or lighting up the carvings strange and rare,
That told of patient toil, and reverent care ;
Ivy that trembled on the spray, and ears
Of heavy corn, and slender bulrush spears,
And all the thousand tangled weeds that grow
In summer, where the silver rivers flow ;
And demon-heads grotesque, that seemed to glare
In impotent wrath on all the beauty there :
Then the gold rays up pillared shaft would climb
And so be drawn to heaven, at evening time.
And deeper silence, darker shadows flowed
On all around, only the windows glowed
With blazoned glory, like the shields of light
Archangels bear, who, armed with love and might.
Watch upon heaven's battlements at night.
Then all was shade ; the silver lamps that gleamed,

Lost in the daylight, in the darkness seemed
Like sparks of fire in the dim aisles to shine,
Or trembling stars before each separate shrine.
Grown half afraid, the child would leave them there,
And come out, blinded by the noisy glare
That burst upon him from the busy square.

The church was thus his home for rest or play ;
And as he came and went again each day,
The pictured faces that he knew so well,
Seemed to smile on him welcome and farewell.
But holier, and dearer far than all,
One sacred spot his own he loved to call ;
Save at mid-day, half-hidden by the gloom ;
The people call it The White Maiden's Tomb :
For there she stands ; her folded hands are pressed
Together, and laid softly on her breast,
As if she waited but a word to rise
From the dull earth, and pass to the blue skies ;
Her lips expectant part, she holds her breath,
As listening for the angel voice of death.
None know how many years have seen her so,
Or what the name of her who sleeps below.
And here the child would come, and strive to trace,
Through the dim twilight, the pure gentle face
He loved so well, and here he oft would bring
Some violet blossom of the early spring ;
And climbing softly by the fretted stand,
Not to disturb her, lay it in her hand :
Or, whispering a soft loving message sweet,

Would stoop and kiss the little marble feet.
So, when the organ's pealing music rang,
He thought amid the gloom the Maiden sang;
With reverent simple faith by her he knelt,
And fancied what she thought, and what she felt.
"Glory to God," re-echoed from her voice,
And then his little spirit would rejoice;
Or when the Requiem sobbed upon the air,
His baby tears dropped with her mournful prayer.

So years fled on, while childish fancies past,
The childish love and simple faith could last.
The artist-soul awoke in him, the flame
Of genius, like the light of Heaven, came
Upon his brain, and (as it will, if true)
It touched his heart and lit his spirit, too.
His father saw, and with a proud content
Let him forsake the toil where he had spent
His youth's first years, and on one happy day
Of pride, before the old man passed away,
He stood with quivering lips, and the big tears
Upon his cheek, and heard the dream of years
Living and speaking to his very heart—
The low hushed murmur at the wondrous art
Of him, who with young trembling fingers made
The great church-organ answer as he played;
And, as the uncertain sound grew full and strong,
Rush with harmonious spirit-wings along,
And thrill with master-power the breathless throng.

The old man died, and years passed on, and still

The young musician bent his heart and will
To his dear toil. St. Bavon now had grown
More dear to him, and even more his own ;
And as he left it every night he prayed
A moment by the archway in the shade,
Kneeling once more within the sacred gloom
Where the White Maiden watched upon her tomb.
His hopes of travel and a world-wide fame,
Cold Time had sobered, and his fragile frame ;
Content at last only in dreams to roam,
Away from the tranquillity of home ;
Content that the poor dwellers by his side
Saw in him but the gentle friend and guide,
The patient counsellor in the poor strife
And petty details of their common life,
Who comforted where woe and grief might fall,
Nor slighted any pain or want as small,
But whose great heart took in and felt for all.

Still he grew famous—many came to be
His pupils in the art of harmony.
One day a voice floated so pure and free
Above his music, that he turned to see
What angel sang, and saw before his eyes,
What made his heart leap with a strange surprise,
His own White Maiden, calm, and pure, and mild,
As in his childish dreams she sang and smiled ;
Her eyes raised up to Heaven, her lips apart,
And music overflowing from her heart.
But the faint blush that tinged her cheek betrayed

No marble statue, but a living maid;
Perplexed and startled at his wondering look,
Her rustling score of Mozart's Sanctus shook;
The uncertain notes, like birds within a snare,
Fluttered and died upon the trembling air.

Days passed; each morning saw the maiden stand,
Her eyes cast down, her lesson in her hand,
Eager to study, never weary, while
Repaid by the approving word or smile
Of her kind master; days and months fled on;
One day the pupil from the choir was gone;
Gone to take light, and joy, and youth once more,
Within the poor musician's humble door;
And to repay, with gentle happy art,
The debt so many owed his generous heart.
And now, indeed, was one who knew and felt
That a great gift of God within him dwelt;
One who could listen, who could understand,
Whose idle work dropped from her slackened hand,
While with wet eyes entranced she stood, nor knew
How the melodious wingèd hours flew;
Who loved his art as none had loved before,
Yet prized the noble tender spirit more.
While the great organ brought from far and near
Lovers of harmony to praise and hear,
Unmarked by aught save what filled every day,
Duty, and toil, and rest, years passed away :
And now by the low archway in the shade
Beside her mother knelt a little maid,

Who, through the great cathedral learned to roam,
Climb to the choir, and bring her father home ;
And stand, demure and solemn by his side,
Patient till the last echo softly died ;
Then place her little hand in his, and go
Down the dark winding stair to where below
The mother knelt, within the gathering gloom
Waiting and praying by the Maiden's Tomb.

So their life went, until, one winter's day,
Father and child came there alone to pray—
The mother, gentle soul, had fled away !
Their life was altered now, and yet the child
Forgot her passionate grief in time, and smiled,
Half wondering why, when spring's fresh breezes came,
To see her father was no more the same.
Half guessing at the shadow of his pain,
And then contented if he smiled again,
A sad cold smile, that passed in tears away,
As re-assured she ran once more to play.
And now each year that added grace to grace,
Fresh bloom and sunshine to the young girl's face,
Brought a strange light in the musician's eyes,
As if he saw some starry hope arise,
Breaking upon the midnight of sad skies.
It might be so: more feeble year by year,
The wanderer to his resting-place drew near.
One day the Gloria he could play no more,
Echoed its grand rejoicing as of yore ;
His hands were clasped, his weary head was laid,

Upon the tomb where the White Maiden prayed:
Where the child's love first dawned, his soul first spoke,
The old man's heart there throbbed its last and broke.
The grave cathedral that had nursed his youth,
Had helped his dreaming, and had taught him truth,
Had seen his boyish grief and baby tears,
And watched the sorrows and the joys of years,
Had lit his fame and hope with sacred rays,
And consecrated sad and happy days—
Had blessed his happiness, and soothed his pain,
Now took her faithful servant home again.

He rests in peace: some travellers mention yet
An organist whose name they all forget.
He has a holier and a nobler fame
By poor men's hearths, who love and bless the name
Of a kind friend; and in low tones to-day,
Speak tenderly of him who passed away.
Too poor to help the daughter of their friend,
They grieved to see the little pittance end;
To see her toil and strive with cheerful heart,
To bear the lonely orphan's struggling part;
They grieved to see her go at last alone
To English kinsmen she had never known:
And here she came; the foreign girl soon found
Welcome, and love, and plenty all around,
And here she pays it back with earnest will,
By well-taught housewife watchfulness and skill;
Deep in her heart she holds her father's name,
And tenderly and proudly keeps his fame;

And while she works with thrifty Belgian care,
Past dreams of childhood float upon the air;
Some strange old chant, or solemn Latin hymn,
That echoed through the old cathedral dim,
When as a little child each day she went
To kneel and pray by an old tomb in Ghent.

THE ANGEL OF DEATH.

WHY shouldst thou fear the beautiful angel,
        Death,
   Who waits thee at the portals of the skies,
Ready to kiss away thy struggling breath,
   Ready with gentle hand to close thine eyes?

How many a tranquil soul has passed away,
   Fled gladly from fierce pain and pleasures dim,
To the eternal splendour of the day;
   And many a troubled heart still calls for him.

Spirits too tender for the battle here
   Have turned from life, its hopes, its fears, its charms;
And children, shuddering at a world so drear,
   Have smiling passed away into his arms.

He whom thou fearest will, to ease its pain,
   Lay his cold hand upon thy aching heart:

Will soothe the terrors of thy troubled brain,
  And bid the shadow of earth's grief depart.

He will give back what neither time, nor might,
  Nor passionate prayer, nor longing hope restore,
(Dear as to long blind eyes recovered sight,)
  He will give back those who are gone before.

Oh, what were life, if life were all? Thine eyes
  Are blinded by their tears, or thou wouldst see
Thy treasures wait thee in the far-off skies,
  And Death, thy friend, will give them all to thee.

A DREAM.

ALL yesterday I was spinning,
    Sitting alone in the sun;
  And the dream that I spun was so
      lengthy,
  It lasted till day was done.

I heeded not cloud or shadow
    That flitted over the hill,
Or the humming-bees, or the swallows,
    Or the trickling of the rill.

I took the threads for my spinning,
    All of blue summer air,

And a flickering ray of sunlight
  Was woven in here and there.

The shadows grew longer and longer,
  The evening wind passed by,
And the purple splendour of sunset
  Was flooding the western sky.

But I could not leave my spinning,
  For so fair my dream had grown,
I heeded not, hour by hour,
  How the silent day had flown.

At last the grey shadows fell round me,
  And the night came dark and chill,
And I rose and ran down the valley,
  And left it all on the hill.

I went up the hill this morning
  To the place where my spinning lay—
There was nothing but glistening dewdrops
  Remained of my dream to-day.

THE PRESENT.

DO not crouch to-day, and worship
   The old Past, whose life is fled,
   Hush your voice to tender reverence;
Crowned he lies, but cold and dead:
For the Present reigns our monarch,
   With an added weight of hours;
Honour her, for she is mighty!
   Honour her, for she is ours!

See the shadows of his heroes
   Girt around her cloudy throne;
Every day the ranks are strengthened
   By great hearts to him unknown;
Noble things the great Past promised,
   Holy dreams, both strange and new;
But the Present shall fulfil them,
   What he promised, she shall do.

She inherits all his treasures,
   She is heir to all his fame,
And the light that lightens round her
   Is the lustre of his name;
She is wise with all his wisdom,
   Living on his grave she stands,

On her brow she bears his laurels,
  And his harvest in her hands.

Coward, can she reign and conquer
  If we thus her glory dim?
Let us fight for her as nobly
  As our fathers fought for him.
God, who crowns the dying ages,
  Bids her rule, and us obey—
Bids us cast our lives before her,
  Bids us serve the great To-day.

CHANGES.

MOURN, O rejoicing heart!
    The hours are flying;
    Each one some treasure takes,
  Each one some blossom breaks,
    And leaves it dying;
  The chill dark night draws near,
    Thy sun will soon depart,
    And leave thee sighing;
  Then mourn, rejoicing heart,
    The hours are flying!

Rejoice, O grieving heart!
    The hours fly fast;

With each some sorrow dies,
With each some shadow flies,
   Until at last
The red dawn in the east
    Bids weary night depart,
    And pain is past.
    Rejoice then, grieving heart,
    The hours fly fast!

STRIVE, WAIT, AND PRAY.

S TRIVE; yet I do not promise
   The prize you dream of to-day
   Will not fade when you think to
      grasp it,
And melt in your hand away;
But another and holier treasure,
   You would now perchance disdain,
Will come when your toil is over,
   And pay you for all your pain.

Wait; yet I do not tell you
   The hour you long for now,
Will not come with its radiance vanished
   And a shadow upon its brow;
Yet far through the misty future,
   With a crown of starry light,
An hour of joy you know not
   Is winging her silent flight.

Pray ; though the gift you ask for
　　May never comfort your fears,
May never repay your pleading,
　　Yet pray, and with hopeful tears ;
An answer, not that you long for,
　　But diviner, will come one day ;
Your eyes are too dim to see it,
　　Yet strive, and wait, and pray.

A LAMENT FOR THE SUMMER.

MOAN, oh ye Autumn Winds !
　　Summer has fled,
　　The flowers have closed their tender leaves
　　　　and die ;
　　The Lily's gracious head
All low must lie,
　　Because the gentle Summer now is dead.

　Grieve, oh ye Autumn Winds !
　　Summer lies low ;
The rose's trembling leaves will soon be shed,
　　For she that loved her so,
Alas, is dead !
　　And one by one her loving children go.

Wail, oh ye Autumn Winds !
   She lives no more,
The gentle Summer, with her balmy breath,
   Still sweeter than before
When nearer death,
   And brighter every day the smile she wore !

Mourn, mourn, oh Autumn Winds,
   Lament and mourn ;
How many half-blown buds must close and die ;
   Hopes with the Summer born
All faded lie,
   And leave us desolate and Earth forlorn !

THE UNKNOWN GRAVE.

NO name to bid us know
      Who rests below,
   No word of death or birth,
   Only the grass's wave,
Over a mound of earth,
   Over a nameless grave.

Did this poor wandering heart
   In pain depart ?
Longing, but all too late,
   For the calm home again,

Where patient watchers wait,
  And still will wait in vain.

Did mourners come in scorn,
  And thus forlorn,
Leave him, with grief and shame,
  To silence and decay,
And hide the tarnished name
  Of the unconscious clay ?

It may be from his side
  His loved ones died,
And last of some bright band,
  (Together now once more,)
He sought his home, the land
  Where they had gone before.

No matter—limes have made
  As cool a shade,
And lingering breezes pass
  As tenderly and slow,
As if beneath the grass
  A monarch slept below.

No grief, though loud and deep,
  Could stir that sleep ;
And earth and heaven tell
  Of rest that shall not cease,
Where the cold world's farewell
  Fades into endless peace.

GIVE ME THY HEART.

WITH echoing steps the worshippers
    Departed one by one ;
  The organ's pealing voice was stilled,
    The vesper hymn was done ;
The shadows fell from roof and arch,
    Dim was the incensed air,
One lamp alone with trembling ray,
    Told of the Presence there !

In the dark church she knelt alone ;
    Her tears were falling fast ;
" Help, Lord," she cried, " the shades of death
    Upon my soul are cast !
Have I not shunned the path of sin,
    And chosen the better part ? "
What voice came through the sacred air ?—
    " *My child, give me thy Heart !* "

" Have I not laid before Thy shrine
    My wealth, oh Lord ? " she cried ;
" Have I kept aught of gems or gold,
    To minister to pride ?
Have I not bade youth's joys retire,
    And vain delights depart ? "—
But sad and tender was the voice—
    " *My child, give me thy Heart !* "

" Have I not, Lord, gone day by day
  Where Thy poor children dwell ;
And carried help, and gold, and food ?
  Oh Lord, Thou knowest it well !
From many a house, from many a soul,
  My hand bids care depart :"—
More sad, more tender, was the voice—
  " *My child, give me thy Heart !* "

" Have I not worn my strength away
  With fast and penance sore ?
Have I not watched and wept ? " she cried ;
  " Did Thy dear Saints do more ?
Have I not gained Thy grace, oh Lord,
  And won in Heaven my part ?"—
It echoed louder in her soul—
  " *My child, give me thy Heart !*

" For I have loved thee with a love
  No mortal heart can show ;
A love so deep, my Saints in heaven
  Its depths can never know :
When pierced and wounded on the Cross,
  Man's sin and doom were mine,
I loved thee with undying love,
  Immortal and divine !

" I loved thee ere the skies were spread ;
  My soul bears all thy pains ;
To gain thy love my sacred Heart
  In earthly shrines remains :

Vain are thy offerings, vain thy sighs,
  Without one gift divine,
Give it, my child, thy Heart to me,
  And it shall rest in mine ! "

In awe she listened, and the shade
  Passed from her soul away ;
In low and trembling voice she cried—
  " Lord, help me to obey !
Break Thou the chains of earth, oh Lord,
  That bind and hold my heart ;
Let it be Thine, and Thine alone,
  Let none with Thee have part.

" Send down, oh Lord, Thy sacred fire !
  Consume and cleanse the sin
That lingers still within its depths :
  Let heavenly love begin.
That sacred flame Thy Saints have known,
  Kindle, oh Lord, in me,
Thou above all the rest for ever,
  And all the rest in Thee."

The blessing fell upon her soul ;
  Her angel by her side
Knew that the hour of peace was come;
  Her soul was purified :
The shadows fell from roof and arch,
  Dim was the incensed air—
But Peace went with her as she left
  The sacred Presence there !

THE WAYSIDE INN.

A LITTLE past the village
The Inn stood, low and white;
Green shady trees behind it,
And an orchard on the right;
Where over the green paling
The red-cheeked apples hung,
As if to watch how wearily
The sign-board creaked and swung.

The heavy-laden branches,
Over the road hung low,
Reflected fruit or blossom
From the wayside well below;
Where children, drawing water,
Looked up and paused to see,
Amid the apple-branches,
A purple Judas Tree.

The road stretched winding onward
For many a weary mile—
So dusty foot-sore wanderers
Would pause and rest awhile;
And panting horses halted,
And travellers loved to tell

The quiet of the wayside inn,
  The orchard, and the well.

Here Maurice dwelt; and often
  The sunburnt boy would stand
Gazing upon the distance,
  And shading with his hand
His eyes, while watching vainly
  For travellers, who might need
His aid to loose the bridle,
  And tend the weary steed.

And once (the boy remembered
  That morning, many a day—
The dew lay on the hawthorn,
  The bird sang on the spray)
A train of horsemen, nobler
  Than he had seen before,
Up from the distance gallopped.
  And halted at the door.

Upon a milk-white pony,
  Fit for a faery queen,
Was the loveliest little damsel
  His eyes had ever seen :
A serving-man was holding
  The leading rein, to guide
The pony and its mistress,
  Who cantered by his side.

Her sunny ringlets round her
   A golden cloud had made,
While her large hat was keeping
   Her calm blue eyes in shade;
One hand held fast the silken reins
   To keep her steed in check,
The other pulled his tangled mane,
   Or stroked his glossy neck.

And as the boy brought water,
   And loosed the rein, he heard
The sweetest voice that thanked him
   In one low gentle word;
She turned her blue eyes from him,
   Looked up, and smiled to see
The hanging purple blossoms
   Upon the Judas Tree;

And showed it with a gesture,
   Half pleading, half command,
Till he broke the fairest blossom,
   And laid it in her hand;
And she tied it to her saddle
   With a ribbon from her hair,
While her happy laugh rang gaily,
   Like silver on the air.

But the champing steeds were rested---
   The horsemen now spurred on,

And down the dusty highway
  They vanished and were gone.
Years passed, and many a traveller
  Paused at the old inn-door,
But the little milk-white pony
  And the child returned no more.

Years passed, the apple-branches
  A deeper shadow shed;
And many a time the Judas Tree,
  Blossom and leaf, lay dead;
When on the loitering western breeze
  Came the bells' merry sound,
And flowery arches rose, and flags
  And banners waved around.

Maurice stood there expectant:
  The bridal train would stay
Some moments at the inn-door,
  The eager watchers say;
They come—the cloud of dust draws near—
  'Mid all the state and pride,
He only sees the golden hair
  And blue eyes of the bride.

The same, yet, ah, still fairer;
  He knew the face once more
That bent above the pony's neck
  Years past at that inn-door:

Her shy and smiling eyes looked round,
  Unconscious of the place,
Unconscious of the eager gaze
  He fixed upon her face.

He plucked a blossom from the tree—
  The Judas Tree—and cast
Its purple fragrance towards the Bride,
  A message from the Past.
The signal came, the horses plunged—
  Once more she smiled around :
The purple blossom in the dust
  Lay trampled on the ground.

Again the slow years fleeted,
  Their passage only known
By the height the Passion-flower
  Around the porch had grown ;
And many a passing traveller
  Paused at the old inn-door,
But the bride, so fair and blooming,
  The bride returned no more.

One winter morning, Maurice,
  Watching the branches bare,
Rustling and waving dimly
  In the grey and misty air,
Saw blazoned on a carriage
  Once more the well-known shield,
The stars and azure fleurs-de-lis
  Upon a silver field.

He looked—was that pale woman,
　　So grave, so worn, so sad,
The child, once young and smiling,
　　The bride, once fair and glad?
What grief had dimmed that glory,
　　And brought that dark eclipse
Upon her blue eyes' radiance,
　　And paled those trembling lips?

What memory of past sorrow,
　　What stab of present pain,
Brought that deep look of anguish,
　　That watched the dismal rain,
That watched (with the absent spirit
　　That looks, yet does not see)
The dead and leafless branches
　　Upon the Judas Tree.

The slow dark months crept onward
　　Upon their icy way,
'Till April broke in showers,
　　And Spring smiled forth in May;
Upon the apple-blossoms
　　The sun shone bright again,
When slowly up the highway
　　Came a long funeral train.

The bells tolled slowly, sadly,
　　For a noble spirit fled;

Slowly, in pomp and honour,
    They bore the quiet dead.
Upon a black-plumed charger
    One rode, who held a shield,
Where stars and azure fleurs-de-lis
    Shone on a silver field.

'Mid all that homage given
    To a fluttering heart at rest,
Perhaps an honest sorrow
    Dwelt only in one breast.
One by the inn-door standing
    Watched with fast-dropping tears
The long procession passing,
    And thought of bygone years.

The boyish, silent homage
    To child and bride unknown,
The pitying tender sorrow
    Kept in his heart alone,
Now laid upon the coffin
    With a purple flower, might be
Told to the cold dead sleeper ;—
    The rest could only see
A fragrant purple blossom,
    Plucked from a Judas Tree.

VOICES OF THE PAST.

YOU wonder that my tears should flow
   In listening to that simple strain;
   That those unskilful sounds should fill
My soul with joy and pain—
How can you tell what thoughts it stirs
   Within my heart again?

You wonder why that common phrase,
   So all unmeaning to your ear,
Should stay me in my merriest mood,
   And thrill my soul to hear—
How can you tell what ancient charm
   Has made me hold it dear?

You marvel that I turn away
   From all those flowers so fair and bright.
And gaze at this poor herb, till tears
   Arise and dim my sight—
You cannot tell how every leaf
   Breathes of a past delight.

You smile to see me turn and speak
   With one whose converse you despise;
You do not see the dreams of old
   That with his voice arise—

How can you tell what links have made
  Him sacred in my eyes?

Oh, these are Voices of the Past,
  Links of a broken chain,
Wings that can bear me back to Times
  Which cannot come again—
Yet God forbid that I should lose
  The echoes that remain!

THE DARK SIDE.

THOU hast done well, perhaps,
    To lift the bright disguise,
    And lay the bitter truth
  Before our shrinking eyes;
When evil crawls below
  What seems so pure and fair,
Thine eyes are keen and true
  To find the serpent there:
And yet—I turn away;
  Thy task is not divine—
The evil angels look
  On earth with eyes like thine.

Thou hast done well, perhaps,
To show how closely wound
  Dark threads of sin and self

With our best deeds are found.
How great and noble hearts,
   Striving for lofty aims,
Have still some earthly cord
   A meaner spirit claims;
And yet—although thy task
   Is well and fairly done,
Methinks for such as thou
   There is a holier one.

Shadows there are, who dwell
   Among us, yet apart,
Deaf to the claim of God,
   Or kindly human heart;
Voices of earth and heaven
   Call, but they turn away,
And Love, through such black night,
   Can see no hope of day;
And yet—our eyes are dim,
   And thine are keener far—
Then gaze till thou canst see
   The glimmer of some star.

The black stream flows along
   Whose waters we despise—
Show us reflected there
   Some fragment of the skies;
'Neath tangled thorns and briars,
   (The task is fit for thee,)

Seek for the hidden flowers,
　We are too blind to see;
Then will I thy great gift
　A crown and blessing call;
Angels look thus on men,
　And God sees good in all!

A FIRST SORROW.

ARISE! this day shall shine,
　　For evermore,
　To thee a star divine,
　　On Time's dark shore.

Till now thy soul has been
　All glad and gay:
Bid it awake, and look
　At grief to-day!

No shade has come between
　Thee and the sun;
Like some long childish dream
　Thy life has run:

But now the stream has reached
　A dark, deep sea,
And Sorrow, dim and crowned,
　Is waiting thee.

Each of God's soldiers bears
    A sword divine :
Stretch out thy trembling hands
    To-day for thine !

To each anointed Priest
    God's summons came :
Oh, Soul, he speaks to-day
    And calls thy name.

Then, with slow reverent step,
    And beating heart,
From out thy joyous days,
    Thou must depart.

And, leaving all behind,
    Come forth, alone,
To join the chosen band
    Around the throne.

Raise up thine eyes—be strong,
    Nor cast away
The crown, that God has given
    Thy soul to-day !

MURMURS.

WHY wilt thou make bright music
 Give forth a sound of pain?
Why wilt thou weave fair flowers
 Into a weary chain?

Why turn each cool grey shadow
 Into a world of fears?
Why say the winds are wailing?
 Why call the dewdrops tears?

The voices of happy nature,
 And the Heaven's sunny gleam,
Reprove thy sick heart's fancies,
 Upbraid thy foolish dream.

Listen, and I will tell thee
 The song Creation sings,
From the humming of bees in the heather,
 To the flutter of angels' wings.

An echo rings for ever,
 The sound can never cease;
It speaks to God of glory,
 It speaks to Earth of peace.

H

Not alone did angels sing it
  To the poor shepherd's ear;
But the spherèd Heavens chant it,
  While listening ages hear.

Above thy peevish wailing
  Rises that holy song;
Above Earth's foolish clamour,
  Above the voice of wrong.

No creature of God's too lowly
  To murmur peace and praise:
When the starry nights grow silent,
  Then speak the sunny days.

So leave thy sick heart's fancies,
  And lend thy little voice
To the silver song of glory
  That bids the world rejoice.

GIVE.

SEE the rivers flowing
　　Downwards to the sea,
　　Pouring all their treasures
Bountiful and free—
Yet to help their giving
　　Hidden springs arise;
Or, if need be, showers
　　Feed them from the skies!

Watch the princely flowers
　　Their rich fragrance spread,
Load the air with perfumes,
　　From their beauty shed—
Yet their lavish spending
　　Leaves them not in dearth,
With fresh life replenished
　　By their mother earth!

Give thy heart's best treasures—
　　From fair Nature learn;
Give thy love—and ask not,
　　Wait not a return!
And the more thou spendest
　　From thy little store,
With a double bounty,
　　God will give thee more.

MY JOURNAL.

'T is a dreary evening;
  The shadows rise and fall:
  With strange and ghostly changes,
They flicker on the wall.

Make the charred logs burn brighter;
  I will show you, by their blaze,
The half-forgotten record
  Of bygone things and days.

Bring here the ancient volume;
  The clasp is old and worn,
The gold is dim and tarnished,
  And the faded leaves are torn.

The dust has gathered on it—
  There are so few who care
To read what Time has written
  Of joy and sorrow there.

Look at the first fair pages;
  Yes—I remember all:
The joys now seem so trivial,
  The griefs so poor and small.

Let us read the dreams of glory
　That childish fancy made ;
Turn to the next few pages,
　And see how soon they fade.

Here, where still waiting, dreaming,
　For some ideal Life,
The young heart all unconscious
　Had entered on the strife.

See how this page is blotted :
　What—could those tears be mine ?
How coolly I can read you,
　Each blurred and trembling line.

Now I can reason calmly,
　And, looking back again,
Can see divinest meaning
　Threading each separate pain.

Here strong resolve—how broken ;
　Rash hope, and foolish fear,
And prayers, which God in pity
　Refused to grant or hear.

Nay—I will turn the pages
　To where the tale is told
Of how a dawn diviner
　Flushed the dark clouds with gold.

And see, that light has gilded
    The story—nor shall set ;
And, though in mist and shadow,
    You know I see it yet.

Here—well, it does not matter,
    I promised to read all ;
I know not why I falter,
    Or why my tears should fall ;

You see each grief is noted ;
    Yet it was better so—
I can rejoice to-day—the pain
    Was over, long ago.

I read—my voice is failing,
    But you can understand
How the heart beat that guided
    This weak and trembling hand.

Pass over that long struggle,
    Read where the comfort came,
Where the first time is written
    Within the book your name.

Again it comes, and oftener,
    Linked, as it now must be,
With all the joy or sorrow
    That Life may bring to me.

So all the rest—you know it :
　　Now shut the clasp again,
And put aside the record
　　Of bygone hours of pain.

The dust shall gather on it,
　　I will not read it more :
Give me your hand—what was it
　　We were talking of before?

I know not why—but tell me
　　Of something gay and bright.
It is strange—my heart is heavy,
　　And my eyes are dim to-night.

A CHAIN.

THE bond that links our souls together;
　　Will it last through stormy weather?
　　Will it moulder and decay
As the long hours pass away?
Will it stretch if Fate divide us,
When dark and weary hours have tried us?
Oh, if it look too poor and slight
Let us break the links to-night !

It was not forged by mortal hands,
Or clasped with golden bars and bands,
Save thine and mine, no other eyes
The slender link can recognize :
In the bright light it seems to fade—
And it is hidden in the shade;
While Heaven nor Earth have never heard,
Or solemn vow, or plighted word.

Yet what no mortal hand could make,
No mortal power can ever break ;
What words or vows could never do,
No words or vows can make untrue;
And if to other hearts unknown
The dearer and the more our own,
Because too sacred and divine
For other eyes, save thine and mine.

And see, though slender, it is made
Of Love and Trust, and can they fade?
While, if too slight it seem, to bear
The breathings of the summer air,
We know that it could bear the weight
Of a most heavy heart of late,
And as each day and hour flew
The stronger for its burthen grew.

And, too, we know and feel again
It has been sanctified by pain,
For what God deigns to try with sorrow
He means not to decay to-morrow ;

But through that fiery trial last
When earthly ties and bonds are past ;
What slighter things dare not endure
Will make our Love more safe and pure.

Love shall be purified by Pain,
And Pain be soothed by Love again :
So let us now take heart and go
Cheerfully on, through joy and woe ;
No change the summer sun can bring,
Or the inconstant skies of spring,
Or the bleak winter's stormy weather,
For we shall meet them, Love, together !

THE PILGRIMS.

THE way is long and dreary,
 The path is bleak and bare ;
 Our feet are worn and weary,
But we will not despair.
More heavy was Thy burthen,
More desolate Thy way ;—
Oh Lamb of God who takest
The sin of the world away,
   Have mercy on us.

The snows lie thick around us
In the dark and gloomy night ;

And the tempest wails above us,
And the stars have hid their light;
But blacker was the darkness
Round Calvary's Cross that day;—
Oh Lamb of God who takest
The sin of the world away,
 Have mercy on us.

Our hearts are faint with sorrow,
Heavy and hard to bear;
For we dread the bitter morrow,
But we will not despair :
Thou knowest all our anguish,
And Thou wilt bid it cease,—
Oh Lamb of God who takest
The sin of the world away,
 Give us Thy Peace!

INCOMPLETENESS.

 OTHING resting in its own completeness
Can have worth or beauty : but alone
Because it leads and tends to farther
 sweetness,
Fuller, higher, deeper than its own.

Spring's real glory dwells not in the meaning,
Gracious though it be, of her blue hours ;
But is hidden in her tender leaning
To the Summer's richer wealth of flowers.

Dawn is fair, because the mists fade slowly
Into Day, which floods the world with light ;
Twilight's mystery is so sweet and holy
Just because it ends in starry Night.

Childhood's smiles unconscious graces borrow
From Strife, that in a far-off future lies ;
And angel glances (veiled now by Life's sorrow)
Draw our hearts to some belovèd eyes.

Life is only bright when it proceedeth
Towards a truer, deeper Life above ;
Human Love is sweetest when it leadeth
To a more divine and perfect Love.

Learn the mystery of Progression duly :
Do not call each glorious change, Decay ;
But know we only hold our treasures truly,
When it seems as if they passed away.

Nor dare to blame God's gifts for incompleteness ;
In that want their beauty lies : they roll
Towards some infinite depth of love and sweetness,
Bearing onward man's reluctant soul.

A LEGEND OF BREGENZ.

GIRT round with rugged mountains
  The fair Lake Constance lies ;
In her blue heart reflected
  Shine back the starry skies ;
And, watching each white cloudlet
  Float silently and slow,
You think a piece of Heaven
  Lies on our earth below !

Midnight is there : and Silence,
  Enthroned in Heaven, looks down
Upon her own calm mirror,
  Upon a sleeping town :
For Bregenz, that quaint city
  Upon the Tyrol shore,
Has stood above Lake Constance,
  A thousand years and more.

Her battlements and towers,
  From off their rocky steep,
Have cast their trembling shadow
  For ages on the deep :
Mountain, and lake, and valley,
  A sacred legend know,
Of how the town was saved, one night,
  Three hundred years ago.

Far from her home and kindred,
　　A Tyrol maid had fled,
To serve in the Swiss valleys,
　　And toil for daily bread;
And every year that fleeted
　　So silently and fast,
Seemed to bear farther from her
　　The memory of the Past.

She served kind, gentle masters,
　　Nor asked for rest or change;
Her friends seemed no more new ones,
　　Their speech seemed no more strange;
And when she led her cattle
　　To pasture every day,
She ceased to look and wonder
　　On which side Bregenz lay.

She spoke no more of Bregenz,
　　With longing and with tears;
Her Tyrol home seemed faded
　　In a deep mist of years;
She heeded not the rumours
　　Of Austrian war and strife;
Each day she rose contented,
　　To the calm toils of life.

Yet, when her master's children
　　Would clustering round her stand,
She sang them ancient ballads
　　Of her own native land;

And when at morn and evening
   She knelt before God's throne,
The accents of her childhood
   Rose to her lips alone.

And so she dwelt: the valley
   More peaceful year by year;
When suddenly strange portents,
   Of some great deed seemed near.
The golden corn was bending
   Upon its fragile stalk,
While farmers, heedless of their fields,
   Paced up and down in talk.

The men seemed stern and altered,
   With looks cast on the ground;
With anxious faces, one by one,
   The women gathered round;
All talk of flax, or spinning,
   Or work, was put away;
The very children seemed afraid
   To go alone to play.

One day, out in the meadow
   With strangers from the town,
Some secret plan discussing,
   The men walked up and down.
Yet, now and then seemed watching.
   A strange uncertain gleam,
That looked like lances 'mid the trees,
   That stood below the stream.

At eve they all assembled,
    Then care and doubt were fled ;
With jovial laugh they feasted ;
    The board was nobly spread.
The elder of the village
    Rose up, his glass in hand,
And cried, " We drink the downfall
    " Of an accursed land !

" The night is growing darker,
    " Ere one more day is flown,
" Bregenz, our foemen's stronghold,
    " Bregenz shall be our own ! "
The women shrank in terror,
    (Yet Pride, too, had her part,)
But one poor Tyrol maiden
    Felt death within her heart.

Before her, stood fair Bregenz ;
    Once more her towers arose !
What were the friends beside her ?
    Only her country's foes !
The faces of her kinsfolk,
    The days of childhood flown,
The echoes of her mountains,
    Reclaimed her as their own !

Nothing she heard around her,
    (Though shouts rang forth again,)
Gone were the green Swiss valleys,
    The pasture, and the plain ;

Before her eyes one vision,
　And in her heart one cry,
That said, " Go forth, save Bregenz,
　And then, if need be, die ! "

With trembling haste and breathless,
　With noiseless step she sped ;
Horses and weary cattle
　Were standing in the shed ;
She loosed the strong white charger,
　That fed from out her hand,
She mounted, and she turned his head
　Towards her native land.

Out—out into the darkness—
　Faster, and still more fast ;
The smooth grass flies behind her,
　The chestnut wood is past ;
She looks up ; clouds are heavy :
　Why is her steed so slow ?—
Scarcely the wind beside them,
　Can pass them as they go.

" Faster ! " she cries, " Oh faster ! "
　Eleven the church-bells chime :
" Oh God," she cries, " help Bregenz.
　And bring me there in time ! "
But louder than bells' ringing,
　Or lowing of the kine,
Grows nearer in the midnight
　The rushing of the Rhine.

Shall not the roaring waters
    Their headlong gallop check?
The steed draws back in terror,
    She leans upon his neck
To watch the flowing darkness;
    The bank is high and steep;
One pause—he staggers forward,
    And plunges in the deep.

She strives to pierce the blackness,
    And looser throws the rein;
Her steed must breast the waters
    That dash above his mane.
How gallantly, how nobly,
    He struggles through the foam,
And see—in the far distance,
    Shine out the lights of home!

Up the steep banks he bears her,
    And now, they rush again
Towards the heights of Bregenz,
    That tower above the plain.
They reach the gate of Bregenz,
    Just as the midnight rings,
And out come serf and soldier
    To meet the news she brings.

Bregenz is saved! Ere daylight
    Her battlements are manned;
Defiance greets the army
    That marches on the land.

I

And if to deeds heroic
    Should endless fame be paid,
Bregenz does well to honour
    The noble Tyrol maid.

Three hundred years are vanished,
    And yet upon the hill
An old stone gateway rises,
    To do her honour still.
And there, when Bregenz women
    Sit spinning in the shade,
They see in quaint old carving
    The Charger and the Maid.

And when, to guard old Bregenz,
    By gateway, street, and tower.
The warder paces all night long,
    And calls each passing hour ;
"Nine," "ten," "eleven," he cries aloud,
    And then (Oh crown of Fame !)
When midnight pauses in the skies,
    He calls the maiden's name !

A FAREWELL.

FAREWELL, oh dream of mine!
　　I dare not stay;
The hour is come, and time
　　Will not delay:
Pleasant and dear to me
　　Wilt thou remain;
No future hour
　　Brings thee again.

She stands, the Future dim,
　　And draws me on,
And shows me dearer joys—
　　But thou art gone!
Treasures and Hopes more fair,
　　Bears she for me,
And yet I linger,
　　Oh dream, with thee!

Other and brighter days,
　　Perhaps she brings;
Deeper and holier songs,
　　Perchance she sings;
But thou and I, fair time,
　　We too must sever—
Oh dream of mine,
　　Farewell for ever!

SOWING AND REAPING.

SOW with a generous hand;
    Pause not for toil or pain;
    Weary not through the heat of summer,
  Weary not through the cold spring rain;
But wait till the autumn comes
    For the sheaves of golden grain.

Scatter the seed, and fear not,
    A table will be spread;
What matter if you are too weary
    To eat your hard-earned bread:
Sow, while the earth is broken,
    For the hungry must be fed.

Sow;—while the seeds are lying
    In the warm earth's bosom deep,
And your warm tears fall upon it—
    They will stir in their quiet sleep;
And the green blades rise the quicker,
    Perchance, for the tears you weep.

Then sow;—for the hours are fleeting,
    And the seed must fall to-day;
And care not what hands shall reap it,
    Or if you shall have passed away

Before the waving corn-fields
  Shall gladden the sunny day.

Sow ; and look onward, upward,
  Where the starry light appears—
Where, in spite of the coward's doubting,
  Or your own heart's trembling fears,
You shall reap in joy the harvest
  You have sown to-day in tears.

THE STORM.

    HE tempest rages wild and high,
    The waves lift up their voice and cry
    Fierce answers to the angry sky,—
        Miserere Domine.

Through the black night and driving rain,
A ship is struggling, all in vain
To live upon the stormy main ;—
        Miserere Domine.

The thunders roar, the lightnings glare,
Vain is it now to strive or dare ;
A cry goes up of great despair,—
        Miserere Domine.

The stormy voices of the main,
The moaning wind, and pelting rain
Beat on the nursery window pane :—
   Miserere Domine.

Warm curtained was the little bed,
Soft pillowed was the little head ;
" The storm will wake the child," they said :—
   Miserere Domine.

Cowering among his pillows white
He prays, his blue eyes dim with fright,
" Father, save those at sea to-night ! "—
   Miserere Domine.

The morning shone all clear and gay,
On a ship at anchor in the bay,
And on a little child at play,—
   Gloria tibi Domine !

WORDS.

WORDS are lighter than the cloud-foam
 Of the restless ocean spray ;
Vainer than the trembling shadow
 That the next hour steals away.
By the fall of summer raindrops
 Is the air as deeply stirred ;

And the rose-leaf that we tread on
    Will outlive a word.

Yet, on the dull silence breaking
    With a lightning flash, a Word,
Bearing endless desolation
    On its blighting wings, I heard :
Earth can forge no keener weapon,
    Dealing surer death and pain,
And the cruel echo answered
      Through long years again.

I have known one word hang starlike
    O'er a dreary waste of years,
And it only shone the brighter
    Looked at through a mist of tears ;
While a weary wanderer gathered
    Hope and heart on Life's dark way,
By its faithful promise, shining
      Clearer day by day.

I have known a spirit, calmer
    Than the calmest lake, and clear
As the heavens that gazed upon it,
    With no wave of hope or fear ;
But a storm had swept across it,
    And its deepest depths were stirred.
(Never, never more to slumber,)
      Only by a word.

I have known a word more gentle
　　Than the breath of summer air ;
In a listening heart it nestled,
　　And it lived for ever there.
Not the beating of its prison
　　Stirred it ever, night or day ;
Only with the heart's last throbbing
　　　Could it fade away.

Words are mighty, words are living :
　　Serpents with their venomous stings,
Or bright angels, crowding round us,
　　With heaven's light upon their wings :
Every word has its own spirit,
　　True or false, that never dies ;
Every word man's lips have uttered
　　Echoes in God's skies.

A LOVE TOKEN.

O you grieve no costly offering
　　To the Lady you can make ?
　One there is, and gifts less worthy
Queens have stooped to take.

Take a Heart of virgin silver,
　　Fashion it with heavy blows,

Cast it into Love's hot furnace
    When it fiercest glows.

With Pain's sharpest point transfix it,
    And then carve in letters fair,
Tender dreams and quaint devices,
    Fancies sweet and rare.

Set within it Hope's blue sapphire,
    Many-changing opal fears,
Blood-red ruby-stones of daring,
    Mixed with pearly tears.

And when you have wrought and laboured
    Till the gift is all complete,
You may humbly lay your offering
    At the Lady's feet.

Should her mood perchance be gracious—
    With disdainful smiling pride,
She will place it with the trinkets
    Glittering at her side.

A TRYST WITH DEATH.

I AM footsore and very weary,
    But I travel to meet a Friend :
The way is long and dreary,
    But I know that it soon must end

He is travelling fast like the whirlwind,
  And though I creep slowly on,
We are drawing nearer, nearer,
  And the journey is almost done.

Through the heat of many summers,
  Through many a springtime rain,
Through long autumns and weary winters,
  I have hoped to meet him, in vain.

I know that he will not fail me,
  So I count every hour chime,
Every throb of my own heart's beating,
  That tells of the flight of Time.

On the day of my birth he plighted
  His kingly word to me :—
I have seen him in dreams so often,
  That I know what his smile must be.

I have toiled through the sunny woodland,
  Through fields that basked in the light;
And through the lone paths in the forest
  I crept in the dead of night.

I will not fear at his coming,
  Although I must meet him alone :
He will look in my eyes so gently,
  And take my hand in his own.

Like a dream all my toil will vanish,
　　When I lay my head on his breast—
But the journey is very weary,
　　And he only can give me rest !

FIDELIS.

YOU have taken back the promise
　　That you spoke so long ago ;
　　Taken back the heart you gave me—
I must even let it go.
Where Love once has breathed, Pride dieth:
　　So I struggled, but in vain,
First to keep the links together,
　　Then to piece the broken chain.

But it might not be—so freely
　　All your friendship I restore,
And the heart that I had taken
　　As my own for evermore.
No shade of reproach shall touch you,
　　Dread no more a claim from me—
But I will not have you fancy
　　That I count myself as free.

I am bound by the old promise ;
　　What can break that golden chain ?

Not even the words that you have spoken,
　　Or the sharpness of my pain:
Do you think, because you fail me
　　And draw back your hand to-day,
That from out the heart I gave you
　　My strong love can fade away?

It will live.　No eyes may see it;
　　In my soul it will lie deep,
Hidden from all; but I shall feel it
　　Often stirring in its sleep.
So remember, that the friendship
　　Which you now think poor and vain,
Will endure in hope and patience,
　　Till you ask for it again.

Perhaps in some long twilight hour,
　　Like those we have known of old,
When past shadows gather round you,
　　And your present friends grow cold,
You may stretch your hands out towards me,—
　　Ah! you will—I know not when—
I shall nurse my love and keep it
　　Faithfully, for you, till then.

A SHADOW.

WHAT lack the valleys and mountains
  That once were green and gay?
 What lack the babbling fountains?
  Their voice is sad to-day.
   Only the sound of a voice,
   Tender and sweet and low,
   That made the earth rejoice,
    A year ago!

What lack the tender flowers?
 A shadow is on the sun:
What lack the merry hours,
 That I long that they were done?
   Only two smiling eyes,
   That told of joy and mirth:
   They are shining in the skies,
    I mourn on earth!

What lacks my heart, that makes it
 So weary and full of pain,
That trembling Hope forsakes it,
 Never to come again?
   Only another heart,
   Tender and all mine own,
   In the still grave it lies;
    I weep alone!

THE SAILOR BOY.

MY Life you ask of? why, you know
Full soon my little Life is told;
It has had no great joy or woe,
For I am only twelve years old.
Ere long I hope I shall have been
On my first voyage, and wonders seen.
Some princess I may help to free
From pirates, on a far-off sea:
Or, on some desert isle be left,
Of friends and shipmates all bereft.

For the first time I venture forth,
From our blue mountains of the north.
My kinsman kept the lodge that stood
Guarding the entrance near the wood,
By the stone gateway grey and old,
With quaint devices carved about,
And broken shields; while dragons bold
Glared on the common world without;
And the long trembling ivy spray
Half hid the centuries' decay.
In solitude and silence grand
The castle towered above the land:
The castle of the Earl, whose name
(Wrapped in old bloody legends) came

Down through the times when Truth and Right
Bent down to armèd Pride and Might.
He owned the country far and near;
And, for some weeks in every year,
(When the brown leaves were falling fast
And the long, lingering autumn passed,)
He would come down to hunt the deer,
With hound and horse in splendid pride.
The story lasts the live-long year,
The peasant's winter evening fills,
When he is gone and they abide
In the lone quiet of their hills.

I longed, too, for the happy night,
When, all with torches flaring bright,
The crowding villagers would stand,
A patient, eager, waiting band,
Until the signal ran like flame—
" They come !" and, slackening speed, they came.
Outriders first, in pomp and state,
Pranced on their horses through the gate !
Then the four steeds as black as night,
All decked with trappings blue and white,
Drew through the crowd that opened wide,
The Earl and Countess side by side.
The stern grave Earl, with formal smile
And glistening eyes and stately pride,
Could ne'er my childish gaze beguile
From the fair presence by his side.
The lady's soft sad glance, her eyes,

(Like stars that shone in summer skies,)
Her pure white face so calmly bent,
With gentle greetings round her sent
Her look, that always seemed to gaze
Where the blue past had closed again
Over some happy shipwrecked days,
With all their freight of love and pain :
She did not even seem to see
The little lord upon her knee.
And yet he was like angel fair,
With rosy cheeks and golden hair,
That fell on shoulders white as snow :
But the blue eyes that shone below
His clustering rings of auburn curls
Were not his mother's, but the Earl's.

I feared the Earl, so cold and grim,
I never dared be seen by him.
When through our gate he used to ride,
My kinsman Walter bade me hide ;
He said he was so stern.
So, when the hunt came past our way,
I always hastened to obey,
Until I heard the bugles play
The notes of their return.
But she—my very heart-strings stir
Whene'er I speak or think of her—
The whole wide world could never see
A noble lady such as she,
So full of angel charity.

Strange things of her our neighbours told
In the long winter evenings cold,
Around the fire.   They would draw near
And speak half-whispering, as in fear;
As if they thought the Earl could hear
Their treason 'gainst his name.
They thought the story that his pride
Had stooped to wed a low-born bride,
A stain upon his fame.
Some said 'twas false; there could not be
Such blot on his nobility:
But others vowed that they had heard
The actual story word for word,
From one who well my lady knew,
And had declared the story true.

In a far village, little known,
She dwelt—so ran the tale—alone.
A widowed bride, yet, oh! so bright,
Shone through the mist of grief, her charms;
They said it was the loveliest sight—
She with her baby in her arms.
The Earl, one summer morning, rode
By the sea-shore where she abode;
Again he came—that vision sweet
Drew him reluctant to her feet.
Fierce must the struggle in his heart
Have been, between his love and pride,
Until he chose that wondrous part,
To ask her to become his bride.

K

Yet, ere his noble name she bore,
He made her vow that nevermore
She would behold her child again,
But hide his name and hers from men.
The trembling promise duly spoken,
All links of the low past were broken;
And she arose to take her stand
Amid the nobles of the land.
Then all would wonder—could it be
That one so lowly born as she,
Raised to such height of bliss, should seem
Still living in some weary dream?
'Tis true she bore with calmest grace
The honours of her lofty place,
Yet never smiled, in peace or joy,
Not even to greet her princely boy.
She heard, with face of white despair,
The cannon thunder through the air,
That she had given the Earl an heir.
Nay, even more, (they whispered low,
As if they scarce durst fancy so,)
That, through her lofty wedded life,
No word, no tone, betrayed the wife.
Her look seemed ever in the past;
Never to him it grew more sweet;
The self-same weary glance she cast
Upon the grey-hound at her feet,
As upon him, who bade her claim
The crowning honour of his name.

This gossip, if old Walter heard,
He checked it with a scornful word :
I never durst such tales repeat ;
He was too serious and discreet
To speak of what his lord might do ;
Besides, he loved my lady too.
And many a time, I recollect,
They were together in the wood ;
He, with an air of grave respect,
And earnest look, uncovered stood.
And though their speech I never heard,
(Save now and then a louder word,)
I saw he spake as none but one
She loved and trusted, durst have done ;
For oft I watched them in the shade
That the close forest branches made,
Till slanting golden sunbeams came
And smote the fir-trees into flame,
A radiant glory round her lit,
Then down her white robes seemed to flit,
Gilding the brown leaves on the ground,
And all the waving ferns around.
While by some gloomy pine she leant
And he in earnest talk would stand,
I saw the tear-drops, as she bent,
Fall on the flowers in her hand.—
Strange as it seemed and seems to be,
That one so sad, so cold as she,
Could love a little child like me—
Yet so it was.   I never heard

Such tender words as she would say,
And murmurs, sweeter than a word,
Would breathe upon me as I lay.
While I, in smiling joy, would rest,
For hours, my head upon her breast.
Our neighbours said that none could see
In me the common childish charms,
(So grave and still I used to be,)
And yet she held me in her arms,
In a fond clasp, so close, so tight—
I often dream of it at night.
She bade me tell her all—no other
My childish thoughts e'er cared to know:
For I—I never knew my mother;
I was an orphan long ago.
And I could all my fancies pour,
That gentle loving face before.
She liked to hear me tell her all;
How that day I had climbed the tree,
To make the largest fir-cones fall;
And how one day I hoped to be
A sailor on the deep blue sea—
She loved to hear it all!

Then wondrous things she used to tell,
Of the strange dreams that she had known.
I used to love to hear them well,
If only for her sweet low tone,
Sometimes so sad, although I knew
That such things never could be true.

One day she told me such a tale
It made me grow all cold and pale,
The fearful thing she told !
Of a poor woman mad and wild
Who coined the life-blood of her child,
And tempted by a fiend, had sold
The heart out of her breast for gold.
But, when she saw me frightened seem,
She smiled, and said it was a dream.
When I look back and think of her,
My very heart-strings seem to stir ;
How kind, how fair she was, how good
I cannot tell you.   If I could
You, too, would love her.   The mere thought
Of her great love for me has brought
Tears in my eyes : though far away,
It seems as it were yesterday.
And just as when I look on high
Through the blue silence of the sky,
Fresh stars shine out, and more and more,
Where I could see so few before ;
So, the more steadily I gaze
Upon those far-off misty days,
Fresh words, fresh tones, fresh memories start
Before my eyes and in my heart.
I can remember how one day
(Talking in silly childish way)
I said how happy I should be
If I were like her son—as fair,
With just such bright blue eyes as he,

And such long locks of golden hair.
A strange smile on her pale face broke,
And in strange solemn words she spoke :
" My own, my darling one—no, no !
I love you, far, far better so.
I would not change the look you bear,
Or one wave of your dark brown hair.
The mere glance of your sunny eyes,
Deep in my deepest soul I prize
Above that baby fair !
Not one of all the Earl's proud line
In beauty ever matched with thine ;
And, 'tis by thy dark locks thou art
Bound even faster round my heart,
And made more wholly mine ! "
And then she paused, and weeping said,
" You are like one who now is dead—
Who sleeps in a far-distant grave.
Oh may God grant that you may be
As noble and as good as he,
As gentle and as brave ! "
Then in my childish way I cried,
" The one you tell me of who died,
Was he as noble as the Earl ? "
I see her red lips scornful curl,
I feel her hold my hand again
So tightly, that I shrink in pain—
I seem to hear her say,
" He whom I tell you of, who died,
He was so noble and so gay,

The Sailor Boy.

So generous and so brave,
That the proud Earl by his dear side
Would look a craven slave."
She paused; then, with a quivering sigh,
She laid her hand upon my brow:
" Live like him, darling, and so die.
Remember that he tells you now,
True peace, real honour, and content,
In cheerful pious toil abide ;
That gold and splendour are but sent
To curse our vanity and pride."

One day some childish fever pain
Burnt in my veins and fired my brain
Moaning, I turned from side to side ;
And, sobbing in my bed, I cried,
Till night in calm and darkness crept
Around me, and at last I slept.
When suddenly I woke to see
The Lady bending over me.
The drops of cold November rain
Were falling from her long, damp hair;
Her anxious eyes were dim with pain ;
Yet she looked wondrous fair.
Arrayed for some great feast she came,
With stones that shone and burnt like flame ;
Wound round her neck, like some bright snake,
And set like stars within her hair,
They sparkled so, they seemed to make
A glory everywhere.

I felt her tears upon my face,
Her kisses on my eyes;
And a strange thought I could not **trace**
I felt within my heart arise;
And, half in feverish pain, I said:
" Oh if my mother were not dead !"
And Walter bade me sleep; but she
Said, " Is it not the same to thee
That *I* watch by thy bed ? "
I answered her, " I love you, too;
But it can never be the same;
She was no Countess like to you,
Nor wore such sparkling stones of flame."
Oh the wild look of fear and dread !
The cry she gave of bitter woe !
I often wonder what I said
To make her moan and shudder so.
Through the long night she tended me
With such sweet care and charity.
But I should weary you to tell
All that I know and love so well:
Yet one night more stands out alone
With a sad sweetness all its own.

The wind blew loud that dreary night:
Its wailing voice I well remember;
The stars shone out so large and bright
Upon the frosty fir-boughs white,
That dreary night of cold December.
I saw old Walter silent stand,

Watching the soft white flakes of snow
With looks I could not understand,
Of strange perplexity and woe.
At last he turned and took my hand,
And said the Countess just had sent
To bid us come; for she would fain
See me once more, before she went
Away—never to come again.
We came in silence through the wood
(Our footfall was the only sound)
To where the great white castle stood,
With darkness shadowing it around.
Breathless, we trod with cautious care
Up the great echoing marble stair;
Trembling, by Walter's hand I held,
Scared by the splendours I beheld:
Now thinking, "Should the Earl appear!"
Now looking up with giddy fear
To the dim vaulted roof, that spread
Its gloomy arches overhead.
Long corridors we softly past,
(My heart was beating loud and fast)
And reached the Lady's room at last:
A strange faint odour seemed to weigh
Upon the dim and darkened air;
One shaded lamp, with softened ray,
Scarce showed the gloomy splendour there.
The dull red brands were burning low,
And yet a fitful gleam of light,
Would now and then, with sudden glow,

Start forth, then sink again in night.
I gazed around, yet half in fear,
Till Walter told me to draw near ·
And in the strange and flickering light,
Towards the Lady's bed I crept ;
All folded round with snowy white,
She lay ; (one would have said she slept ;)
So still the look of that white face,
It seemed as it were carved in stone,
I paused before I dared to place
Within her cold white hand my own.
But, with a smile of sweet surprise,
She turned to me her dreamy eyes ;
And slowly, as if life were pain,
She drew me in her arms to lie :
She strove to speak, and strove in vain ;
Each breath was like a long-drawn sigh.
The throbs that seemed to shake her breast,
The trembling clasp, so loose and weak,
At last grew calmer, and at rest ;
And then she strove once more to speak :
" My God, I thank thee, that my pain
Of day by day and year by year,
Has not been suffered all in vain,
And I may die while he is near.
I will not fear but that Thy grace
Has swept away my sin and woe,
And sent this little angel face,
In my last hour to tell me so."
(And here her voice grew faint and low,)

" My child, where'er thy life may go,
To know that thou art brave and true,
Will pierce the highest heavens through,
And even there my soul shall be
More joyful for this thought of thee."
She folded her white hands, and stayed ;
All cold and silently she lay :
I knelt beside the bed, and prayed
The prayer she used to make me say.
I said it many times, and then
She did not move, but seemed to be
In a deep sleep, nor stirred again.
No sound woke in the silent room,
Or broke the dim and solemn gloom,
Save when the brands that burnt so low,
With noisy fitful gleam of light,
Would spread around a sudden glow,
Then sink in silence and in night.
How long I stood I do not know :
At last poor Walter came, and said
(So sadly) that we now must go,
And whispered, she we loved was dead.
He bade me kiss her face once more,
Then led me sobbing to the door.
I scarcely knew what dying meant,
Yet a strange grief, before unknown,
Weighed on my spirit as we went
And left her lying all alone.

We went to the far North once more,

To seek the well-remembered home,
Where my poor kinsman dwelt before,
Whence now he was too old to roam ;
And there six happy years we past,
Happy and peaceful till the last ;
When poor old Walter died, and he
Blessed me and said I now might be
A sailor on the deep blue sea.
And so I go ; and yet in spite
Of all the joys I long to know,
Though I look onward with delight,
With something of regret I go ;
And young or old, on land or sea,
One guiding memory I shall take—
Of what She prayed that I might be,
And what I will be for her sake !

A CROWN OF SORROW.

A SORROW, wet with early tears
    Yet bitter, had been long with me :
I wearied of this weight of years,
    And would be free.

I tore my Sorrow from my heart,
    I cast it far away in scorn ;
Right joyful that we two could part—
    Yet most forlorn.

I sought, (to take my Sorrow's place,)
    Over the world for flower or gem—
But she had had an ancient grace
    Unknown to them.

I took once more with strange delight
    My slighted Sorrow; proudly now,
I wear it, set with stars of light,
    Upon my brow.

THE LESSON OF THE WAR.

(1855.)

THE feast is spread through England
    For rich and poor to-day;
    Greetings and laughter may be there,
  But thoughts are far away;
Over the stormy ocean,
    Over the dreary track,
Where some are gone, whom England
    Will never welcome back.

Breathless she waits, and listens
    For every eastern breeze
That bears upon its bloody wings
    News from beyond the seas.

The leafless branches stirring
   Make many a watcher start ;
The distant tramp of steed may send
   A throb from heart to heart.

The rulers of the nation,
   The poor ones at their gate,
With the same eager wonder
   The same great news await.
The poor man's stay and comfort,
   The rich man's joy and pride,
Upon the bleak Crimean shore
   Are fighting side by side.

The bullet comes—and either
   A desolate hearth may see ;
And God alone to-night knows where
   The vacant place may be !
The dread that stirs the peasant
   Thrills nobles' hearts with fear—
Yet above selfish sorrow
   Both hold their country dear.

The rich man who reposes
   In his ancestral shade,
The peasant at his ploughshare,
   The worker at his trade,
Each one his all has perilled,
   Each has the same great stake,
Each soul can but have patience,
   Each heart can only break !

Hushed is all party clamour;
  One thought in every heart,
One dread in every household,
  Has bid such strife depart.
England has called her children;
  Long silent—the word came
That lit the smouldering ashes
  Through all the land to flame.

Oh you who toil and suffer,
  You gladly heard the call;
But those you sometimes envy
  Have they not given their all?
Oh you who rule the nation,
  Take now the toil-worn hand—
Brothers you are in sorrow,
  In duty to your land.
Learn but this noble lesson
  Ere Peace returns again,
And the life-blood of Old England
  Will not be shed in vain.

THE TWO SPIRITS.

(1855.)

LAST night, when weary silence fell on all,
    And starless skies arose so dim and vast,
    I heard the Spirit of the Present call
Upon the sleeping Spirit of the Past.
Far off and near, I saw their radiance shine,
And listened while they spoke of deeds divine.

The Spirit of the Past.

My deeds are writ in iron;
    My glory stands alone;
A veil of shadowy honour
    Upon my tombs is thrown;
The great names of my heroes
    Like gems in history lie;
To live they deemed ignoble,
    Had they the chance to die!

The Spirit of the Present.

My children, too, are honoured;
    Dear shall their memory be
To the proud lands that own them;
    Dearer than thine to thee;

For, though they hold that sacred
    Is God's great gift of life,
At the first call of duty
    They rush into the strife !

The Spirit of the Past.

Then, with all valiant precepts
    Woman's soft heart was fraught;
" Death, not dishonour," echoed
    The war-cry she had taught.
Fearless and glad, those mothers,
    At bloody deaths elate,
Cried out they bore their children
    Only for such a fate !

The Spirit of the Present.

Though such stern laws of honour
    Are faded now away,
Yet many a mourning mother,
    With nobler grief than they,
Bows down in sad submission :
    The heroes of the fight
Learnt at her knee the lesson,
    " For God and for the Right : "

The Spirit of the Past.

No voice there spake of sorrow :
    They saw the noblest fall

L

With no repining murmur;
    Stern Fate was lord of all.
And when the loved ones perished,
    One cry alone arose,
Waking the startled echoes,
    "Vengeance upon our foes!"

The Spirit of the Present.

Grief dwells in France and England
    For many a noble son;
Yet louder than the sorrow,
    "Thy will, Oh God, be done!"
From desolate homes is rising
    One prayer, "Let carnage cease!
On friends and foes have mercy,
    Oh Lord, and give us peace!"

The Spirit of the Past.

Then, every hearth was honoured
    That sent its children forth,
To spread their country's glory,
    And gain her south or north.
Then, little recked they numbers,
    No band would ever fly,
But stern and resolute they stood
    To conquer or to die.

The Spirit of the Present.

And now from France and England
    Their dearest and their best

Go forth to succour freedom,
　To help the much oppressed ;
Now, let the far-off Future
　And Past bow down to-day,
Before the few young hearts that hold
　Whole armaments at bay.

The Spirit of the Past.

Then, each one strove for honour,
　Each for a deathless name ;
Love, home, rest, joy, were offered
　As sacrifice to Fame.
They longed that in far ages
　Their deeds might still be **told,**
And distant times and nations
　Their names in honour hold.

The Spirit of the Present.

Though nursed by such old legends,
　Our heroes of to-day
Go cheerfully to battle
　As children go to play ;
They gaze with awe and wonder
　On your great names of pride,
Unconscious that their own will shine
　In glory side by side !

Day dawned ; and as the Spirits passed away,
Methought I saw, in the dim morning grey,
The Past's bright diadem had paled before
The starry crown the glorious Present wore.

A LITTLE LONGER.

LITTLE longer yet—a little longer,
    Shall violets bloom for thee, and sweet
        birds sing ;
And the lime branches where soft winds are blowing,
Shall murmur the sweet promise of the Spring !

A little longer yet—a little longer,
Thou shalt behold the quiet of the morn ;
While tender grasses and awakening flowers
Send up a golden mist to greet the dawn !

A little longer yet—a little longer,
The tenderness of twilight shall be thine,
The rosy clouds that float o'er dying daylight,
Nor fade till trembling stars begin to shine.

A little longer yet—a little longer,
Shall starry night be beautiful for thee ;
And the cold moon shall look through the blue silence,
Flooding her silver path upon the sea.

A little longer yet—a little longer,
Life shall be thine ; life with its power to will ;
Life with its strength to bear, to love, to conquer,
Bringing its thousand joys thy heart to fill.

A little longer yet—a little longer,
The voices thou hast loved shall charm thine ear;
And thy true heart, that now beats quick to hear them,
A little longer yet shall hold them dear.

A little longer yet—joy while thou mayest;
Love and rejoice! for time has nought in store:
And soon the darkness of the grave shall bid thee
Love and rejoice and feel and know no more.

A little longer still—Patience, Belovèd:
A little longer still, ere Heaven unroll
The Glory, and the Brightness, and the Wonder,
Eternal, and divine, that waits thy Soul!

A little longer ere Life true, immortal,
(Not this our shadowy Life,) will be thine own;
And thou shalt stand where winged Archangels
        worship,
And trembling bow before the Great White Throne.

A little longer still, and Heaven awaits thee,
And fills thy spirit with a great delight;
Then our pale joys will seem a dream forgotten,
Our Sun a darkness, and our Day a Night.

A little longer, and thy Heart, Belovèd,
Shall beat for ever with a Love divine;
And joy so pure, so mighty, so eternal.
No creature knows and lives, will then be thine.

A little longer yet—and angel voices
Shall ring in heavenly chant upon thine ear ;
Angels and Saints await thee, and God needs thee :
Belovèd, can we bid thee linger here !

GRIEF.

AN ancient enemy have I,
And either he or I must die;
For he never leaveth me,
Never gives my soul relief,
Never lets my sorrow cease,
Never gives my spirit peace—
For mine enemy is Grief !

Pale he is, and sad and stern ;
And whene'er he cometh nigh,
Blue and dim the torches burn,
Pale and shrunk the roses turn ;
While my heart that he has pierced
Many a time with fiery lance,
Beats and trembles at his glance :
Clad in burning steel is he,
All my strength he can defy ;
For he never leaveth me—
And one of us must die !

I have said, "Let ancient sages
Charm me from my thoughts of pain!"
So I read their deepest pages,
And I strove to think—in vain !
Wisdom's cold calm words I tried,
But he was seated by my side :—
Learning I have won in vain ;
She cannot rid me of my pain.

When at last soft sleep comes o'er me,
A cold hand is on my heart ;
Stern sad eyes are there before me ;
Not in dreams will he depart :
And when the same dreary vision
From my weary brain has fled,
Daylight brings the living phantom,
He is seated by my bed,
Bending o'er me all the while,
With his cruel, bitter smile,
Ever with me, ever nigh ;—
And either he or I must die !

Then I said, long time ago,
"I will flee to other climes,
I will leave mine ancient foe !"
Though I wandered far and wide
Still he followed at my side.

And I fled where the blue waters
Bathe the sunny isles of Greece ;

Where Thessalian mountains rise
Up against the purple skies;
Where a haunting memory liveth
In each wood and cave and rill;
But no dream of gods could help me—
He went with me still!

I have been where Nile's broad river
Flows upon the burning sand;
Where the desert monster broodeth,
Where the Eastern palm-trees stand;
I have been where pathless forests
Spread a black eternal shade;
Where the lurking panther hiding
Glares from every tangled glade;
But in vain I wandered wide,
He was always by my side!

Then I fled where snows eternal
Cold and dreary ever lie;
Where the rosy lightnings gleam,
Flashing through the northern sky;
Where the red sun turns again
Back upon his path of pain;—
But a shadowy form was with me—
I had fled in vain!

I have thought, " If I can gaze
Sternly on him he will fade,
For I know that he is nothing

Grief.

But a dim ideal shade."
As I gazed at him the more,
He grew stronger than before !

Then I said, " Mine arm is strong,
I will make him turn and flee :"
I have struggled with him long—
But that could never be !

Once I battled with him so
That I thought I laid him low ;
Then in trembling joy I fled,
While again and still again
Murmuring to myself I said,
" Mine old enemy is dead ! "
And I stood beneath the stars,
When a chill came on my frame,
And a fear I could not name,
And a sense of quick despair
And, lo !—mine enemy was there !

Listen, for my soul is weary,
Weary of its endless woe ;
I have called on one to aid me
Mightier even than my foe.
Strength and hope fail day by day ;
I shall cheat him of his prey ;
Some day soon, I know not when,
He will stab me through and through ;
He has wounded me before,

But my heart can bear no more;
Pray that hour may come to me,
Only then shall I be free ;
Death alone has strength to take me
Where my foe can never be ;
Death, and Death alone, has power
To conquer mine old enemy !

THE TRIUMPH OF TIME.

THE tender delicate Flowers,
    I saw them fanned by a warm western wind,
    Fed by soft summer showers,
Shielded by care, and yet, (oh Fate unkind !)
    Fade in a few short hours.

The gentle and the gay,
Rich in a glorious Future of bright deeds,
    Rejoicing in the day,
Are met by Death, who sternly, sadly leads
    Them far away.

And Hopes, perfumed and bright,
So lately shining, wet with dew and tears,
    Trembling in morning light ;
I saw them change to dark and anxious fears
    Before the night !

I wept that all must die—
"Yet Love," I cried, "doth live, and conquer death—"
And Time passed by,
And breathed on Love, and killed it with his breath
Ere Death was nigh.

More bitter far than all
It was to know that Love could change and die—
Hush ! for the ages call
"The Love of God lives through eternity,
And conquers all ! "

A PARTING.

WITHOUT one bitter feeling let us part—
And for the years in which your love has
shed
A radiance like a glory round my head,
I thank you, yes, I thank you from my heart.

I thank you for the cherished hope of years,
A starry future, dim and yet divine,
Winging its way from Heaven to be mine,
Laden with joy, and ignorant of tears.

I thank you, yes, I thank you even more
That my heart learnt not without love to live,

But gave and gave, and still had more to give,
From an abundant and exhaustless store.

I thank you, and no grief is in these tears;
  I thank you, not in bitterness but truth,
  For the fair vision that adorned my youth
And glorified so many happy years.

Yet how much more I thank you that you tore
  At length the veil your hand had woven away,
  Which hid my idol was a thing of clay,
And false the altar I had knelt before.

I thank you that you taught me the stern truth,
  (None other could have told and I believed,)
  That vain had been my life, and I deceived,
And wasted all the purpose of my youth.

I thank you that your hand dashed down the shrine,
  Wherein my idol worship I had paid;
  Else had I never known a soul was made
To serve and worship only the Divine.

I thank you that the heart I cast away
  On such as you, though broken, bruised and crushed,
  Now that its fiery throbbing is all hushed,
Upon a worthier altar I can lay.

I thank you for the lesson that such love
  Is a perverting of God's royal right,

That it is made but for the Infinite,
And all too great to live except above.

I thank you for a terrible awaking,
   And if reproach seemed hidden in my pain,
   And sorrow seemed to cry on your disdain,
Know that my blessing lay in your forsaking.

Farewell for ever now :—in peace we part ;
   And should an idle vision of my tears
   Arise before your soul in after years—
Remember that I thank you from my heart !

THE GOLDEN GATE.

DIM shadows gather thickly round, and up the
    misty stair they climb,
   The cloudy stair that upward leads to where
   the closèd portals shine,
Round which the kneeling spirits wait the opening of
   the Golden Gate.

And some with eager longing go, still pressing forward,
    hand in hand,
And some with weary step and slow, look back where
   their Belovèd stand—
Yet up the misty stair they climb, led onward by the
   Angel Time.

As unseen hands roll back the doors, the light that
      floods the very air
Is but the shadow from within, of the great glory hidden
      there—
And morn and eve, and soon and late, the shadows pass
      within the gate.

As one by one they enter in, and the stern portals close
      once more,
The halo seems to linger round those kneeling closest
      to the door :
The joy that lightened from that place shines still upon
      the watcher's face.

The faint low echo that we hear of far-off music seems
      to fill
The silent air with love and fear, and the world's
      clamours all grow still,
Until the portals close again, and leave us toiling on in
      pain.

Complain not that the way is long—what road is weary
      that leads there ?
But let the Angel take thy hand, and lead thee up the
      misty stair,
And then with beating heart await, the opening of the
      Golden Gate.

PHANTOMS.

BACK, ye Phantoms of the Past;
   In your dreary caves remain :
   What have I to do with memories
Of a long-forgotten pain?

For my Present is all peaceful,
   And my Future nobly planned :
Long ago Time's mighty billows
   Swept your footsteps from the sand.

Back into your caves; nor haunt me
   With your voices full of woe ;
I have buried grief and sorrow
   In the depths of Long-ago.

See the glorious clouds of morning
   Roll away, and clear and bright
Shine the rays of cloudless daylight—
   Wherefore will ye moan of night?

Never shall my heart be burthered
   With its ancient woe and fears,
I can drive them from my presence,
   I can check these foolish tears.

Back, ye Phantoms; leave, oh leave me
  To a new and happy lot;
Speak no more of things departed;
  Leave me—for I know ye not.

Can it be that 'mid my gladness
  I must ever hear you wail,
Of the grief that wrung my spirit,
  And that made my cheek so pale?

Joy is mine; but your sad voices
  Murmur ever in mine ear:
Vain is all the Future's promise,
  While the dreary Past is here.

Vain, oh worse than vain, the Visions
  That my heart, my life would fill,
If the Past's relentless phantoms
  Call upon me still!

THANKFULNESS.

MY God, I thank Thee who hast
      made
    The Earth so bright;
So full of splendour and of joy,
    Beauty and light;
So many glorious things are here,
    Noble and right!

I thank Thee, too, that Thou hast made
    Joy to abound ;
So many gentle thoughts and deeds
    Circling us round,
That in the darkest spot of Earth
    Some love is found.

I thank Thee *more* that all our joy
    Is touched with pain ;
That shadows fall on brightest hours;
    That thorns remain ;
So that Earth's bliss may be our guide,
    And not our chain.

For Thou who knowest, Lord, how soon
    Our weak heart clings,
Hast given us joys, tender and true,
    Yet all with wings,
So that we see, gleaming on high,
    Diviner things !

I thank Thee, Lord, that Thou hast kept
    The best in store ;
We have enough, yet not too much
    To long for more :
A yearning for a deeper peace,
    Not known before.

I thank Thee, Lord, that here our souls,
    Though amply blest,

M

Can never find, although they seek,
  A perfect rest—
Nor ever shall, until they lean
  On Jesus' breast !

HOME-SICKNESS.

WHERE I am, the halls are gilded,
    Stored with pictures bright and rare;
  Strains of deep melodious music
  Float upon the perfumed air :—
Nothing stirs the dreary silence
  Save the melancholy sea,
Near the poor and humble cottage,
  Where I fain would be !

Where I am, the sun is shining,
  And the purple windows glow,
Till their rich armorial shadows
  Stain the marble floor below :—
Faded Autumn leaves are trembling,
  On the withered jasmine tree,
Creeping round the little casement,
  Where I fain would be !

Where I am, the days are passing
  O'er a pathway strewn with flowers ;

Song and joy and starry pleasures
  Crown the happy smiling hours:—
Slowly, heavily, and sadly,
  Time with weary wings must flee,
Marked by pain, and toil, and sorrow,
  Where I fain would be!

Where I am, the great and noble
  Tell me of renown and fame,
And the red wine sparkles highest,
  To do honour to my name :—
Far away a place is vacant,
  By a humble hearth, for me,
Dying embers dimly show it,
  Where I fain would be!

Where I am, are glorious dreamings,
  Science, genius, art divine ;
And the great minds whom all honour
  Interchange their thoughts with mine:—
A few simple hearts are waiting,
  Longing, wearying, for me,
Far away where tears are falling,
  Where I fain would be!

Where I am, all think me happy,
  For so well I play my part,
None can guess, who smile around me,
  How far distant is my heart—

Far away, in a poor cottage,
   Listening to the dreary sea,
Where the treasures of my life are,
   Where I fain would be !

WISHES.

ALL the fluttering wishes
   Caged within thy heart
   Beat their wings against it,
   Longing to depart,
Till they shake their prison
   With their wounded cry;
Open wide thy heart to-day,
   And let the captives fly.

Let them first fly upward
   Through the starry air,
Till you almost lose them,
   Far their home is there ;
Then, with outspread pinions,
   Circling round and round,
Wing their way, wherever
   Want and woe are found.

Where the weary stitcher
   Toils for daily bread ;

Where the lonely watcher
  Watches by her dead ;
Where with thin weak fingers,
  Toiling at the loom,
Stand the little children,
  Blighted ere they bloom.

Where, by darkness blinded,
  Groping for the light,
With distorted conscience
  Men do wrong for right ;
Where, in the cold shadow,
  By smooth pleasure thrown,
Human hearts by hundreds
  Harden into stone.

Where on dusty highways,
  With faint heart and slow,
Cursing the glad sunlight,
  Hungry outcasts go :
Where all mirth is silenced,
  And the hearth is chill,
For one place is empty,
  And one voice is still.

Some hearts will be lighter
  While your captives roam:
For their tender singing,
  Then recall them home ;

When the sunny hours
Into night depart,
Softly they will nestle
In a quiet heart.

THE PEACE OF GOD.

WE ask for Peace, oh Lord!
　　Thy children ask Thy Peace;
Not what the world calls rest,
　That toil and care should cease,
That through bright sunny hours
　Calm Life should fleet away,
And tranquil night should fade
　In smiling day;—
It is not for such Peace that we would pray

We ask for Peace, oh Lord!
　Yet not to stand secure,
Girt round with iron Pride,
　Contented to endure:
Crushing the gentle strings
　That human hearts should know,
Untouched by others' joy
　Or others' woe;—
Thou, oh dear Lord, wilt never teach us so.

We ask Thy Peace, oh Lord !
   Through storm, and fear, and strife,
To light and guide us on,
   Through a long struggling life :
While no success or gain
   Shall cheer the desperate fight,
Or nerve, what the world calls,
     Our wasted might :—
Yet pressing through the darkness to the light.

It is Thine own, oh Lord,
   Who toil while others sleep ;
Who sow with loving care
   What other hands shall reap :
They lean on Thee entranced,
   In calm and perfect rest :
Give us that Peace, oh Lord,
     Divine and blest,
Thou keepest for those hearts who love Thee best.

LIFE IN DEATH AND DEATH IN LIFE.

I.

IF the dread day that calls thee hence,
   Through a red mist of fear should loom,
   (Closing in deadliest night and gloom
Long hours of aching dumb suspense,)
   And leave me to my lonely doom.

I think, belovèd, I could see
   In thy dear eyes the loving light
   Glaze into vacancy and night,
And still say, "God is good to me,
   And all that He decrees is right."

That, watching thy slow struggling breath,
   And answering each imperfect sign,
   I still could pray thy prayer and mine,
And tell thee, dear, though this was death,
   That God was love, and love divine.

Could hold thee in my arms, and lay
   Upon my heart thy weary head,
   And meet thy last smile ere it fled ;
Then hear, as in a dream, one say,
   "Now all is over,—she is dead."

Could smooth thy garments with fond care,
   And cross thy hands upon thy breast,
   And kiss thine eyelids down to rest,
And yet say no word of despair,
   But, through my sobbing, " It is best."

Could stifle down the gnawing pain,
   And say, " We still divide our life,
   She has the rest, and I the strife,
And mine the loss, and hers the gain :
   My ill with bliss for her is rife."

Then turn, and the old duties take—
  Alone now—yet with earnest will
  Gathering sweet sacred traces still
To help me on, and, for thy sake,
  My heart and life and soul to fill.

I think I could check vain weak tears,
  And toil,—although the world's great space
  Held nothing but one vacant place,
And see the dark and weary years
  Lit only by a vanished grace.

And sometimes, when the day was o'er,
  Call up the tender past again :
  Its painful joy, its happy pain,
And live it over yet once more,
  And say, " But few more years remain."

And then, when I had striven my best,
  And all around would smiling say,
"See how Time makes all grief decay,"
Would lie down thankfully to rest,
  And seek thee in eternal day.

II.

But if the day should ever rise—
  It could not and it cannot be—
  Yet, if the sun should ever see,
Looking upon us from his skies,
  A day that took thy heart from me ;

If loving thee still more and more,
    And still so willing to be blind,
    I should the bitter knowledge find,
That Time had eaten out the core
    Of love, and left the empty rind;

If the poor lifeless words, at last,
    (The soul gone, that was once so sweet,)
    Should cease my eager heart to cheat,
And crumble back into the past,
    And show the whole a vain deceit;

If I should see thee turn away,
    And know that prayer, and time, and pain,
    Could no more thy lost love regain,
Than bid the hours of dying day
    Gleam in their mid-day noon again;

If I should loose thy hand, and know
    That henceforth we must dwell apart,
    Since I had seen thy love depart,
And only count the hours flow
    By the dull throbbing of my heart;

If I should gaze and gaze in vain
    Into thine eyes so deep and clear,
    And read the truth of all my fear
Half mixed with pity for my pain,
    And sorrow for the vanished year;

If not to grieve thee overmuch,
   I strove to counterfeit disdain,
   And weave me a new life again,
Which thy life could not mar, or touch,
   And so smile down my bitter pain ;

The ghost of my dead Past would rise
   And mock me, and I could not dare
   Look to a future of despair,
Or even to the eternal skies,
   For I should still be lonely there.

All Truth, all Honour, then would seem
   Vain clouds, which the first wind blew by ;
   All Trust, a folly doomed to die ;
All Life, a useless empty dream ;
   All Love—since thine had failed—a lie.

But see, thy tender smile has cast
   My fear away: this thought of mine
   Is treason to my Love and thine ;
For Love is Life, and Death at last
   Crowns it eternal and divine !

RECOLLECTIONS.

AS strangers, you and I are here ;
   We both as aliens stand,
    Where once, in years gone by, I dwelt
  No stranger in the land.
Then while you gaze on park and stream,
  Let me remain apart,
And listen to the awakened sound
  Of voices in my heart.

Here, where upon the velvet lawn
  The cedar spreads its shade,
And by the flower-beds all around,
  Bright roses bloom and fade ;
Shrill merry childish laughter rings,
  And baby voices sweet,
And by me, on the path, I hear
  The tread of little feet.

Down the dark avenue of limes,
  Whose perfume loads the air,
Whose boughs are rustling overhead,
  (For the west wind is there,)
I hear the sound of earnest talk,
  Warnings and counsels wise,
And the quick questioning that brought
  Such gentle calm replies.

Still the light bridge hangs o'er the lake,
  Where broad-leaved lilies lie,
And the cool water shows again
  The cloud that moves on high ;—
And one voice speaks, in tones I thought
  The past for ever kept ;
But now I know, deep in my heart
  Its echoes only slept.

I hear, within the shady porch,
  Once more, the measured sound
Of the old ballads that were read,
  While we sat listening round :
The starry passion-flower still
  Up the green trellice climbs ;
The tendrils waving seem to keep
  The cadence of the rhymes.

I might have striven, and striven in vain,
  Such visions to recall,
Well known and yet forgotten ; now
  I see, I hear, them all !
The Present pales before the Past,
  Who comes with angel wings ;
As in a dream I stand, amidst
  Strange yet familiar things !

Enough ; so let us go, mine eyes
  Are blinded by their tears ;

A voice speaks to my soul to-day
  Of long forgotten years.
And yet the vision in my heart,
  In a few hours more,
Will fade into the silent past,
  Silently as before.

ILLUSION.

WHERE the golden corn is bending,
  And the singing reapers pass,
Where the chestnut woods are sending
Leafy showers upon the grass,

The blue river onward flowing
  Mingles with its noisy strife,
The murmur of the flowers growing,
  And the hum of insect life.

I, from that rich plain was gazing
  Towards the snowy mountains high,
Who their gleaming peaks were raising
  Up against the purple sky.

And the glory of their shining,
  Bathed in clouds of rosy light,
Set my weary spirit pining
  For a home so pure and bright!

So I left the plain, and weary,
    Fainting, yet with hope sustained,
Toiled through pathways long and dreary
    Till the mountain top was gained.

Lo ! the height that I had taken,
    As so shining from below,
Was a desolate, forsaken
    Region of perpetual snow.

I am faint, my feet are bleeding,
    All my feeble strength is worn,
In the plain no soul is heeding,
    I am here alone, forlorn.

Lights are shining, bells are tolling,
    In the busy vale below ;
Near me night's black clouds are rolling,
    Gathering o'er a waste of snow.

So I watch the river winding
    Through the misty fading plain,
Bitter are the tear-drops blinding,
    Bitter useless toil and pain—
Bitterest of all the finding
    That my dream was false and vain !

A VISION.

GLOOMY and black are the cypress trees,
  Drearily waileth the chill night breeze.
   The long grass waveth, the tombs are white,
And the black clouds flit o'er the chill moonlight.
Silent is all save the dropping rain,
When slowly there cometh a mourning train,
The lone churchyard is dark and dim,
And the mourners raise a funeral hymn :

  " Open, dark grave, and take her ;
    Though we have loved her so,
  Yet we must now forsake her,
  Love will no more awake her :
      (Oh, bitter woe !)
  Open thine arms and take her
      To rest below !

  " Vain is our mournful weeping,
    Her gentle life is o'er ;
  Only the worm is creeping,
  Where she will soon be sleeping,
      For evermore—
  Nor joy nor love is keeping
      For her in store !"

A Vision.

Gloomy and black are the cypress trees,
And drearily wave in the chill night breeze.
The dark clouds part and the heavens are blue,
Where the trembling stars are shining through.
Slowly across the gleaming sky,
A crowd of white angels are passing by.
Like a fleet of swans they float along,
Or the silver notes of a dying song.
Like a cloud of incense their pinions rise,
Fading away up the purple skies.
But hush! for the silent glory is stirred,
By a strain such as earth has never heard:

> " Open, oh Heaven! we bear her,
>   This gentle maiden mild,
> Earth's griefs we gladly spare her,
> From earthly joys we tear her,
>   Still undefiled ;
> And to thine arms we bear her,
>   Thine own, thy child.
>
> " Open, oh Heaven! no morrow
>   Will see this joy o'ercast,
> No pain, no tears, no sorrow,
> Her gentle heart will borrow ;
>   Sad life is past ;
> Shielded and safe from sorrow,
>   At home at last."

But the vision faded and all was still,

On the purple valley and distant hill.
No sound was there save the wailing breeze,
The rain, and the rustling cypress trees.

PICTURES IN THE FIRE.

WHAT is it you ask me, darling?
　　All my stories, child, you know;
　　I have no strange dreams to tell you,
Pictures I have none to show.

Tell you glorious scenes of travel?
　　Nay, my child, that cannot be,
I have seen no foreign countries,
　　Marvels none on land or sea.

Yet strange sights in truth I witness,
　　And I gaze until I tire;
Wondrous pictures, changing ever
　　As I look into the fire.

There, last night, I saw a cavern,
　　Black as pitch; within it lay
Coiled in many folds a dragon,
　　Glaring as if turned at bay.

And a knight in dismal armour
　　On a wingèd eagle came,

To do battle with this dragon;
    And his crest was all of flame.

As I gazed the dragon faded,
    And, instead, sate Pluto crowned,
By a lake of burning fire;
    Spirits dark were crouching round.

That was gone, and lo! before me,
    A cathedral vast and grim;
1 could almost hear the organ
    Peal along the arches dim.

As I watched the wreathèd pillars,
    Groves of stately palms arose.
And a group of swarthy Indians
    Stealing on some sleeping foes.

Stay; a cataract glancing brightly,
    Dashed and sparkled; and beside
Lay a broken marble monster,
    Mouth and eyes were staring wide.

Then I saw a maiden wreathing
    Starry flowers in garlands sweet;
Did she see the fiery serpent
    That was wrapped about her feet?

That fell crashing all and vanished;
    And I saw two armies close—
I could almost hear the clarions,
    And the shouting of the foes.

They were gone; and lo! bright angels,
    On a barren mountain wild,
Raised appealing arms to Heaven,
    Bearing up a little child.

And I gazed, and gazed, and slowly
    Gathered in my eyes sad tears,
And the fiery pictures bore me
    Back through distant dreams of years.

Once again I tasted sorrow,
    With past joy was once more gay,
Till the shade had gathered round me—
    And the fire had died away.

THE SETTLERS.

TWO stranger youths in the Far West,
    Beneath the ancient forest trees,
    Pausing, amid their toil to rest,
Spake of their home beyond the seas;
Spake of the hearts that beat so warmly,
    Of the hearts they loved so well,
In their chilly northern country.
    "Would," they cried, "some voice could tell
Where they are, our own beloved ones!"
    They looked up to the evening sky

Half hidden by the giant branches.
　But heard no angel-voice reply.
All silent was the quiet evening ;
　Silent were the ancient trees ;
They only heard the murmuring song
　　Of the summer breeze,
　That gently played among
　　The acacia trees.

And did no warning spirit answer,
　Amid the silence all around ;
" Before the lowly village altar
　She thou lovest may be found,
Thou, who trustest still so blindly,
　Know she stands a smiling bride !
Forgetting thee, she turneth kindly
　To the stranger at her side.
Yes, this day thou art forgotten,
　Forgotten, too, thy last farewell,
All the vows that she has spoken,
　And thy heart has kept so well.
Dream no more of a starry future,
　In thy home beyond the seas !"
But he only heard the gentle sigh
　　Of the summer breeze,
　So soft.y passing by
　　The acacia trees.

And vainly, too, the other, looking
　Smiling up through hopeful tears,

Asked in his heart of hearts, "Where is she,
    She I love these many years?"
He heard no echo calling faintly:
    "Lo, she lieth cold and pale,
And her smile so calm and saintly
    Heeds not grieving sob or wail—
Heeds not the lilies strewn upon her,
    Pure as she is, and as white,
Or the solemn chanting voices,
    Or the taper's ghastly light."
But silent still was the ancient forest,
    Silent were the gloomy trees,
He only heard the wailing sound
        Of the summer breeze,
    That sadly played around
        The acacia trees!

HUSH!

CAN scarcely hear," she murmured,
    "For my heart beats loud and fast,
    But surely, in the far, far distance,
I can hear a sound at last."
    "It is only the reapers singing,
        As they carry home their sheaves,
    And the evening breeze has risen,
        And rustles the dying leaves."

"Listen ! there are voices talking."
　　Calmly still she strove to speak,
Yet her voice grew faint and trembling,
　　And the red flushed in her cheek.
　　　　" It is only the children playing
　　　　　　Below, now their work is done,
　　　　And they laugh that their eyes are dazzled
　　　　　　By the rays of the setting sun."

Fainter grew her voice, and weaker
　　As with anxious eyes she cried,
" Down the avenue of chestnuts,
　　I can hear a horseman ride."
　　　　" It was only the deer that were feeding
　　　　　　In a herd on the clover grass,
　　　　They were startled, and fled to the thicket,
　　　　　　As they saw the reapers pass."

Now the night arose in silence,
　　Birds lay in their leafy nest,
And the deer couched in the forest,
　　And the children were at rest :
　　　　There was only a sound of weeping
　　　　　　From watchers around a bed,
　　　　But Rest to the weary spirit,
　　　　　　Peace to the quiet Dead !

HOURS.

WHEN the bright stars came out last night,
And the dew lay on the flowers,
I had a vision of delight—
A dream of by-gone hours.

Those hours that came and fled so fast,
Of pleasure or of pain,
As phantoms rose from out the past
Before my eyes again.

With beating heart did I behold
A train of joyous hours,
Lit with the radiant light of old,
And, smiling, crowned with flowers.

And some were hours of childish sorrow,
A mimicry of pain,
That through their tears looked for a morrow
They knew must smile again.

Those hours of hope that longed for life,
And wished their part begun,
And ere the summons to the strife,
Dreamed that the field was won.

I knew the echo of their voice,
  The starry crowns they wore;
The vision made my soul rejoice
  With the old thrill of yore.

I knew the perfume of their flowers;
  The glorious shining rays
Around these happy smiling hours
  Were lit in by-gone days.

Oh stay, I cried—bright visions, stay,
  And leave me not forlorn!
But, smiling still, they passed away,
  Like shadows of the morn.

One spirit still remained, and cried,
  "Thy soul shall ne'er forget!"
He standeth ever by my side—
  The phantom called Regret!

But still the spirits rose, and there
  Were weary hours of pain,
And anxious hours of fear and care
  Bound by an iron chain.

Dim shadows came of lonely hours,
  That shunned the light of day,
And in the opening smile of flowers
  Saw only quick decay.

Calm hours that sought the starry skies
    For heavenly lore were there ;
With folded hands and earnest eyes
    I knew the hours of prayer.

Stern hours that darkened the sun's light,
    Heralds of coming woes,
With trailing wings, before my sight
    From the dim past arose.

As each dark vision passed and spoke
    I prayed it to depart :
At each some buried sorrow woke
    And stirred within my heart.

Until these hours of pain and care
    Lifted their tearful eyes,
Spread their dark pinions in the air
    And passed into the skies.

THE TWO INTERPRETERS.

THE clouds are fleeting by, father,
    Look in the shining west,
    The great white clouds sail onward
Upon the sky's blue breast.

Look at a snowy eagle,
　　His wings are tinged with red,
And a giant dolphin follows him,
　　With a crown upon his head ! "

The father spake no word, but watched
　　The drifting clouds roll by ;
He traced a misty vision too
　　Upon the shining sky ;
A shadowy form, with well-known grace
　　Of weary love and care,
Above the smiling child she held,
　　Shook down her floating hair.

" The clouds are changing now, father,
　　Mountains rise higher and higher!
And see where red and purple ships
　　Sail in a sea of fire ! "
The father pressed the little hand
　　More closely in his own,
And watched a cloud-dream in the sky
　　That he could see alone :
Bright angels carrying far away
　　A white form, cold and dead,
Two held the feet, and two bore up
　　The flower-crowned, drooping head.

"See, father, see ! a glory floods
　　The sky, and all is bright,

And clouds of every hue and shade
  Burn in the golden light.
And now, above an azure lake,
  Rise battlements and towers,
Where knights and ladies climb the heights,
  All bearing purple flowers."

The father looked, and, with a pang
  Of love and strange alarm,
Drew close the little eager child
  Within his sheltering arm;
From out the clouds the mother looks
  With wistful glance below,
She seems to seek the treasure left
  On earth so long ago;
She holds her arms out to her child,
  His cradle-song she sings:
The last rays of the sunset gleam
  Upon her outspread wings.

Calm twilight veils the summer sky.
  The shining clouds are gone:
In vain the merry laughing child
  Still gaily prattles on;
In vain the bright stars, one by one,
  On the blue silence start,
A dreary shadow rests to-night
  Upon the father's heart.

COMFORT.

HAST thou o'er the clear heaven of thy soul
        Seen tempests roll?
    Hast thou watched all the hopes thou wouldst
        have won
        Fade, one by one?
Wait till the clouds are past, then raise thine eyes
        To bluer skies.

Hast thou gone sadly through a dreary night,
        And found no light,
No guide, no star, to cheer thee through the plain—
        No friend, save pain?
Wait, and thy soul shall see, when most forlorn,
        Rise a new morn.

Hast thou beneath another's stern control
        Bent thy sad soul,
And wasted sacred hopes and precious tears?
        Yet calm thy fears,
For thou canst gain, even from the bitterest part,
        A stronger heart.

Has Fate o'erwhelmed thee with some sudden blow?
        Let thy tears flow;

But know when storms are past, the heavens appear
      More pure, more clear ;
And hope, when farthest from their shining rays,
      For brighter days.

Hast thou found life a cheat, and worn in vain
      Its iron chain ?
Has thy soul bent beneath earth's heavy bond?
      Look thou beyond ;
If life is bitter—*there* for ever shine
      Hopes more divine.

Art thou alone, and does thy soul complain
      It lives in vain?
Not vainly does he live who **can** endure.
      Oh be thou sure,
That he who hopes and suffers here, can earn
      A sure return.

Hast thou found nought within thy troubled life
      Save inward strife ?
Hast thou found all she promised thee, Deceit,
      And Hope a cheat?
Endure, and there shall dawn within thy breast
      Eternal rest !

HOME AT LAST.

CHILD, do not fear;
  We shall reach our home to-night,
    For the sky is clear,
  And the waters bright;
And the breezes have scarcely strength
  To unfold that little cloud,
    That like a shroud
  Spreads out its fleecy length;
    Then have no fear,
As we cleave our silver way
    Through the waters clear.

    Fear not, my child!
Though the waves are white and high,
  And the storm blows wild
    Through the gloomy sky;
On the edge of the western sea,
  See that line of golden light,
    Is the haven bright
Where home is awaiting thee;
    Where, this peril past,
We shall rest from our stormy voyage
    In peace at last.

Be not afraid ;
But give me thy hand, and see
How the waves have made
A cradle for thee.
Night is come, dear, and we shall rest ;
So turn from the angry skies,
And close thine eyes,
And lay thy head on my breast :
Child, do not weep ;
In the calm, cold, purple depths
There we shall sleep.

UNEXPRESSED.

DWELLS within the soul of every Artist
More than all his effort can express ;
And he knows the best remains unuttered
Sighing at what *we* call his success.

Vainly he may strive ; he dare not tell us
All the sacred mysteries of the skies :
Vainly he may strive ; the deepest beauty
Cannot be unveiled to mortal eyes.

And the more devoutly that he listens,
And the holier message that is sent,
Still the more his soul must struggle vainly
Bowed beneath a noble discontent.

No great Thinker ever lived and taught you
All the wonder that his soul received;
No true Painter ever set on canvas
All the glorious vision he conceived.

No Musician ever held your spirit
Charmed and bound in his melodious chains,
But be sure he heard, and strove to render,
Feeble echoes of celestial strains.

No real Poet ever wove in numbers
All his dream; but the diviner part,
Hidden from all the world, spake to him only
In the voiceless silence of his heart.

So with Love: for Love and Art united
Are twin mysteries; different, yet the same:
Poor indeed would be the love of any
Who could find its full and perfect name.

Love may strive, but vain is the endeavour
All its boundless riches to enfold;
Still its tenderest, truest secret lingers
Ever in its deepest depths untold.

Things of Time have voices: speak and perish.
Art and Love speak—but their words must be
Like sighings of illimitable forests,
And waves of an unfathomable sea.

BECAUSE.

T is not because your heart is mine—mine
only—
Mine alone;
It is not because you chose me, weak and lonely,
For your own;
Not because the earth is fairer, and the skies
Spread above you
Are more radiant for the shining of your eyes—
That I love you!

It is not because the world's perplexèd meaning
Grows more clear;
And the Parapets of Heaven, with angels leaning,
Seem more near;
And Nature sings of praise with all her voices
Since yours spoke,
Since within my silent heart, that now rejoices,
Love awoke!

Nay, not even because your hand holds heart and life;
At your will
Soothing, hushing all its discord, making strife
Calm and still;

Teaching Trust to fold her wings, nor ever roam
      From her nest ;
Teaching Love that her securest, safest home
      Must be Rest.

But because this human Love, though true and sweet—
      Yours and mine—
Has been sent by Love more tender, more complete,
      More divine ;
That it leads our hearts to rest at last in Heaven,
      Far above you ;
Do I take you as a gift that God has given—
      —And I love you !

REST AT EVENING.

HEN the weariness of Life is ended,
    And the task of our long day is done,
    And the props, on which our hearts depended,
All have failed or broken, one by one ;
Evening and our Sorrow's shadow blended
Telling us that peace is now begun.

How far back will seem the sun 's first dawning,
And those early mists so cold and grey !
Half forgotten even the toil of morning,
And the heat and burthen of the day :

Flowers that we were tending, and weeds scorning,
All alike withered and cast away.

Vain will seem the impatient heart, which waited
Toils that gathered but too quickly round ;
And the childish joy, so soon elated
At the path we thought none else had found ;
And the foolish ardour, soon abated
By the storm which cast us to the ground.

Vain those pauses on the road, each seeming
As our final home and resting-place ;
And the leaving them, while tears were streaming
Of eternal sorrow down our face ;
And the hands we held, fond folly dreaming
That no future could their touch efface.

All will then be faded :—night will borrow
Stars of light to crown our perfect rest ;
And the dim vague memory of faint sorrow
Just remain to show us all was best,
Then melt into a divine to-morrow :—
Oh, how poor a day to be so blest !

A RETROSPECT.

FROM this fair point of present bliss,
   Where we together stand,
   Let me look back once more, and trace
   That long and desert land,
Wherein till now was cast my lot, and I could live, and
      thou wert not.

Strange that my heart could beat, and know
   Alternate joy and pain,
That suns could roll from east to west,
   And clouds could pass in rain,
And the slow hours without thee fleet, nor stay their
      noiseless silver feet.

What had I then? a Hope, that grew
   Each hour more bright and dear,
The flush upon the eastern skies
   That showed the sun was near:—
Now night has faded far away, my sun has risen, and
      it is day.

A dim Ideal of tender grace
   In my soul reigned supreme;
Too noble and too sweet I thought
   To live, save in a dream—
Within thy heart to-day it lies, and looks on me from
      thy dear eyes.

Some gentle spirit—Love I thought—
    Built many a shrine of pain ;
Though each false Idol fell to dust,
    The worship was not vain,
But a faint radiant shadow cast back from our Love
      upon the Past.

And Grief, too, held her vigil there ;
    With unrelenting sway
Breaking my cloudy visions down,
    Throwing my flowers away :—
I owe to her fond care alone that I may now be all
      thine own.

Fair Joy was there—her fluttering wings
    At times she strove to raise ;
Watching through long and patient nights,
    Listening long eager days :
I know now that her heart and mine were waiting,
      Love, to welcome thine.

Thus I can read thy name throughout,
    And, now her task is done,
Can see that even that faded Past
    Was thine, belovèd one,
And so rejoice my Life may be all consecrated, dear,
      to thee.

TRUE OR FALSE.

S O you think you love me, do you?
　　Well, it may be so;
　But there are many ways of loving
　I have learnt to know.
Many ways, and but one true way,
　Which is very rare;
And the counterfeits look brightest,
　Though they will not wear.

Yet they ring, almost, quite truly,
　Last (with care) for long;
But in time must break, may shiver
　At a touch of wrong:
Having seen what looked most real
　Crumble into dust;
Now I chose that test and trial
　Should precede my trust.

I have seen a love demanding
　Time and hope and tears,
Chaining all the past, exacting
　Bonds from future years;
Mind and heart, and joy and sorrow,
　Claiming as its fee:
That was Love of Self, and never,
　Never Love of me!

I have seen a love forgetting
    All above, beyond,
Linking every dream and fancy
    In a sweeter bond ;
Counting every hour worthless,
    Which was cold or free :—
That, perhaps, was—Love of Pleasure,
    But not Love of me !

I have seen a love whose patience
    Never turned aside,
Full of tender, fond devices ;
    Constant, even when tried ;
Smallest boons were held as victories,
    Drops that swelled the sea :
That I think was—Love of Power,
    But not Love of me !

I have seen a love disdaining
    Ease and pride and fame,
Burning even its own white pinions
    Just to feed its flame ;
Reigning thus, supreme, triumphant,
    By the soul's decree ;
That was—Love of Love, I fancy,
    But not Love of me !

I have heard—or dreamt, it may be–
    What Love is when true ;
How to test and how to try it,
    Is the gift of few :

These few say (or did I dream it?)
 That true Love abides
In these very things, but always
 Has a soul besides.

Lives among the false loves, knowing
 Just their peace and strife:
Bears the self-same look, but always
 Has an inner life.
Only a true heart can find it,
 True as it is true,
Only eyes as clear and tender
 Look it through and through.

If it dies, it will not perish
 By Time's slow decay,
True Love only grows (they tell me)
 Stronger, day by day:
Pain—has been its friend and comrade;
 Fate—it can defy;
Only by its own sword, sometimes
 Love can choose to die.

And its grave shall be more noble
 And more sacred still,
Than a throne, where one less worthy
 Reigns and rules at will.
Tell me then, do you dare offer
 This true Love to me? . . .
Neither you nor I can answer;
 We will—wait and see!

GOLDEN WORDS.

OME words are played on golden
strings,
Which I so highly rate,
I cannot bear for meaner things
Their sound to desecrate.

For every day they are not meet,
Or for a careless tone;
They are for rarest, and most sweet,
And noblest use alone.

One word is POET: which is flung
So carelessly away,
When such as you and I have sung,
We hear it, day by day.

Men pay it for a tender phrase
Set in a cadenced rhyme:
I keep it as a crown of praise
To crown the kings of time.

And LOVE: the slightest feelings, stirred
By trivial fancy, seek
Expression in that golden word
They tarnish while they speak.

Nay, let the heart's slow, rare decree,
   That word in reverence keep;
Silence herself should only be
   More sacred and more deep.

FOR EVER : men have grown at length
   To use that word, to raise
Some feeble protest into strength,
   Or turn some tender phrase.

It should be said in awe and fear
   By true heart and strong will,
And burn more brightly year by year,
   A starry witness still.

HONOUR : all trifling hearts are fond
   Of that divine appeal,
And men, upon the slightest bond,
   Set it as slighter seal.

That word should meet a noble foe
   Upon a noble field,
And echo—like a deadly blow
   Turned by a silver shield.

Trust me, the worth of words is such
   They guard all noble things,
And that this rash irreverent touch
   Has jarred some golden strings.

For what the lips have lightly said
   The heart will lightly hold,
And things on which we daily tread
   Are lightly bought and sold.

The sun of every day will bleach
   The costliest purple hue,
And so our common daily speech
   Discolours what was true.

But as you keep some thoughts apart
   In sacred honoured care,
If in the silence of your heart,
   Their utterance too be rare:

Then, while a thousand words repeat
   Unmeaning clamours all,
Melodious golden echoes sweet
   Shall answer when you call.

A LEGEND OF PROVENCE.

THE lights extinguished, by the hearth I leant,
Half weary with a listless discontent.
The flickering giant-shadows, gathering near,
Closed round me with a dim and silent fear.
All dull, all dark; save when the leaping flame,
Glancing, lit up a Picture's ancient frame.

Above the hearth it hung. Perhaps the night,
My foolish tremors, or the gleaming light,
Lent power to that Portrait dark and quaint—
A Portrait such as Rembrandt loved to paint—
The likeness of a Nun. I seemed to trace
A world of sorrow in the patient face,
In the thin hands folded across her breast—
Its own and the room's shadow hid the rest.
I gazed and dreamed, and the dull embers stirred,
Till an old legend that I once had heard
Came back to me ; linked to the mystic gloom
Of that dark Picture in the ghostly room.

In the far south, where clustering vines are hung ;
Where first the old chivalric lays were sung,
Where earliest smiled that gracious child of France,
Angel and knight and fairy, called Romance,
I stood one day. The warm blue June was spread
Upon the earth ; blue summer overhead,
Without a cloud to fleck its radiant glare,
Without a breath to stir its sultry air.
All still, all silent, save the sobbing rush
Of rippling waves, that lapsed in silver hush
Upon the beach ; where, glittering towards the strand,
The purple Mediterranean kissed the land.

All still, all peaceful ; when a convent chime
Broke on the mid-day silence for a time,
Then trembling into quiet, seemed to cease,
In deeper silence and more utter peace.

So as I turned to gaze, where gleaming white,
Half hid by shadowy trees from passers' sight,
The Convent lay, one who had dwelt for long
In that fair home of ancient tale and song,
Who knew the story of each cave and hill,
And every haunting fancy lingering still
Within the land, spake thus to me, and told
The Convent's treasured Legend, quaint and old:

Long years ago, a dense and flowering wood,
Still more concealed where the white convent stood,
Borne on its perfumed wings the title came:
"Our Lady of the Hawthorns" is its name.
Then did that bell, which still rings out to-day,
Bid all the country rise, or eat, or pray.
Before that convent shrine, the haughty knight
Passed the lone vigil of his perilous fight;
For humbler cottage strife or village brawl,
The Abbess listened, prayed, and settled all.
Young hearts that came, weighed down by love or
        wrong,
Left her kind presence comforted and strong.
Each passing pilgrim, and each beggar's right
Was food, and rest, and shelter for the night.
But, more than this, the Nuns could well impart
The deepest mysteries of the healing art;
Their store of herbs and simples was renowned,
And held in wondering faith for miles around.
Thus strife, love, sorrow, good and evil fate,
Found help and blessing at the convent gate.

Of all the nuns, no heart was half so light,
No eyelids veiling glances half as bright,
No step that glided with such noiseless feet,
No face that looked so tender or so sweet,
No voice that rose in choir so pure, so clear,
No heart to all the others half so dear,
So surely touched by others' pain or woe,
(Guessing the grief her young life could not know,)
No soul in childlike faith so undefiled,
As Sister Angela's, the "Convent Child."
For thus they loved to call her.   She had known
No home, no love, no kindred, save their own.
An orphan, to their tender nursing given,
Child, plaything, pupil, now the Bride of Heaven.
And she it was who trimmed the lamp's red light
That swung before the altar, day and night ;
Her hands it was whose patient skill could trace
The finest broidery, weave the costliest lace ;
But most of all, her first and dearest care,
The office she would never miss or share,
Was every day to weave fresh garlands sweet,
To place before the shrine at Mary's feet.
Nature is bounteous in that region fair,
For even winter has her blossoms there.
Thus Angela loved to count each feast the best,
By telling with what flowers the shrine was dressed.
In pomp supreme the countless Roses passed,
Battalion on battalion thronging fast.
Each with a different banner, flaming bright,
Damask, or striped, or crimson, pink, or white,

Until they bowed before a new born queen,
And the pure virgin Lily rose serene.
Though Angela always thought the Mother blest
Must love the time of her own hawthorn best,
Each evening through the year, with equal care,
She placed her flowers ; then kneeling down in prayer,
As their faint perfume rose before the shrine,
So rose her thoughts, as pure and as divine.
She knelt until the shades grew dim without,
Till one by one the altar lights shone out,
Till one by one the Nuns, like shadows dim,
Gathered around to chant their vesper hymn ;
Her voice then led the music's wingèd flight,
And " Ave, Maris Stella " filled the night.

But wherefore linger on those days of peace ?
When storms draw near, then quiet hours must cease.
War, cruel war, defaced the land, and came
So near the convent with its breath of flame,
That, seeking shelter, frightened peasants fled,
Sobbing out tales of coming fear and dread.
Till after a fierce skirmish, down the road,
One night came straggling soldiers, with their load
Of wounded, dying comrades ; and the band,
Half pleading, yet as if they could command,
Summoned the trembling Sisters, craved their care,
Then rode away, and left the wounded there.
But soon compassion bade all fear depart,
And bidding every Sister do her part,
Some prepare simples, healing salves, or bands,

The Abbess chose the more experienced hands,
To dress the wounds needing most skilful care ;
Yet even the youngest Novice took her share
To Angela, who had but ready will
And tender pity, yet no special skill,
Was given the charge of a young foreign Knight,
Whose wounds were painful, but whose danger slight
Day after day she watched beside his bed,
And first in hushed repose the hours fled :
His feverish moans alone the silence stirred,
Or her soft voice, uttering some pious word.
At last the fever left him ; day by day
The hours, no longer silent, passed away.
What could she speak of ? First, to still his plaints,
She told him legends of the martyred Saints ;
Described the pangs, which, through God's plenteous
      grace,
Had gained their souls so high and bright a place.
This pious artifice soon found success—
Or so she fancied—for he murmured less.
So she described the glorious pomp sublime,
In which the chapel shone at Easter time,
The Banners, Vestments, gold, and colours bright,
Counted how many tapers gave their light ;
Then, in minute detail went on to say,
How the High Altar looked on Christmas-day :
The kings and shepherds, all in green and red,
And a bright star of jewels overhead.
Then told the sign by which they all had seen,
How even nature loved to greet her Queen,

For, when Our Lady's last procession went
Down the long garden, every head was bent,
And, rosary in hand, each Sister prayed ;
As the long floating banners were displayed,
They struck the hawthorn boughs, and showers and
          showers
Of buds and blossoms strewed her way with flowers.
The Knight unwearied listened ; till at last,
He too described the glories of his past ;
Tourney, and joust, and pageant bright and fair,
And all the lovely ladies who were there.
But half incredulous she heard.   Could this—
This be the world ? this place of love and bliss !
Where then was hid the strange and hideous charm,
That never failed to bring the gazer harm ?
She crossed herself, yet asked, and listened still,
And still the Knight described with all his skill
The glorious world of joy, all joys above,
Transfigured in the golden mist of love.
Spread, spread your wings, ye angel guardians bright,
And shield these dazzling phantoms from her sight !
But no ; days passed, matins and vespers rang,
And still the quiet Nuns toiled, prayed, and sang,
And never guessed the fatal, coiling net
Which every day drew near, and nearer yet,
Around their darling ; for she went and came
About her duties, outwardly the same.
The same ? ah, no ! even when she knelt to pray,
Some charmèd dream kept all her heart away.
So days went on, until the convent gate

Opened one night.   Who durst go forth so late?
Across the moonlit grass, with stealthy tread,
Two silent, shrouded figures passed and fled.
And all was silent, save the moaning seas,
That sobbed and pleaded, and a wailing breeze
That sighed among the perfumed hawthorn trees.

What need to tell that dream so bright and brief,
Of joy unchequered by a dread of grief?
What need to tell how all such dreams must fade,
Before the slow, foreboding, dreaded shade,
That floated nearer, until pomp and pride,
Pleasure and wealth, were summoned to her side,
To bid, at least, the noisy hours forget,
And clamour down the whispers of regret.
Still Angela strove to dream, and strove in vain ;
Awakened once, she could not sleep again.
She saw, each day and hour, more worthless grown
The heart for which she cast away her own ;
And her soul learnt, through bitterest inward strife,
The slight, frail love for which she wrecked her life,
The phantom for which all her hope was given,
The cold bleak earth for which she bartered heaven
But all in vain ; would even the tenderest heart
Now stoop to take so poor an outcast's part?

Years fled, and she grew reckless more and more,
Until the humblest peasant closed his door,
And where she passed, fair dames, in scorn and pride,
Shuddered, and drew their rustling robes aside.

At last a yearning seemed to fill her soul,
A longing that was stronger than control :
Once more, just once again, to see the place
That knew her young and innocent ; to retrace
The long and weary southern path ; to gaze
Upon the haven of her childish days ;
Once more beneath the convent roof to lie ;
Once more to look upon her home—and die !

Weary and worn—her comrades, chill remorse
And black despair, yet a strange silent force
Within her heart, that drew her more and more—
Onward she crawled, and begged from door to door.
Weighed down with weary days, her failing strength
Grew less each hour, till one day's dawn at length,
As first its rays flooded the world with light,
Showed the broad waters, glittering blue and bright,
And where, amid the leafy hawthorn wood,
Just as of old the quiet cloister stood.
Would any know her ? Nay, no fear.   Her face
Had lost all trace of youth, of joy, of grace,
Of the pure happy soul they used to know—
The novice Angela—so long ago.
She rang the convent bell.   The well-known sound
Smote on her heart, and bowed her to the ground,
And she, who had not wept for long dry years,
Felt the strange rush of unaccustomed tears ;
Terror and anguish seemed to check her breath,
And stop her heart.   Oh God ! could this be death ?
Crouching against the iron gate, she laid

Her weary head against the bars, and prayed :
But nearer footsteps drew, then seemed to wait ;
And then she heard the opening of the grate,
And saw the withered face, on which awoke
Pity and sorrow, as the portress spoke,
And asked the stranger's bidding : " Take me in,"
She faltered, " Sister Monica, from sin,
And sorrow, and despair, that will not cease ;
Oh, take me in, and let me die in peace !"
With soothing words the Sister bade her wait,
Until she brought the key to unbar the gate.
The beggar tried to thank her as she lay,
And heard the echoing footsteps die away.
But what soft voice was that which sounded near,
And stirred strange trouble in her heart to hear?
She raised her head ; she saw—she seemed to know —
A face that came from long, long years ago :
Herself; yet not as when she fled away,
The young and blooming novice, fair and gay,
But a grave woman, gentle and serene :
The outcast knew it—*what she might have been.*
But, as she gazed and gazed, a radiance bright
Filled all the place with strange and sudden light ;
The Nun was there no longer, but instead,
A figure with a circle round its head,
A ring of glory ; and a face, so meek,
So soft, so tender. . . . Angela strove to speak,
And stretched her hands out, crying, " Mary mild,
Mother of mercy, help me !—help your child ! "
And Mary answered, " From thy bitter past,

Welcome, my child ! oh, welcome home at last !
I filled thy place.   Thy flight is known to none,
For all thy daily duties I have done ;
Gathered thy flowers, and prayed, and sung, and slept;
Didst thou not know, poor child, *thy place was kept?*
Kind hearts are here ; yet would the tenderest one
Have limits to its mercy : God has none.
And man's forgiveness may be true and sweet,
But yet he stoops to give it.   More complete
Is Love that lays forgiveness at thy feet,
And pleads with thee to raise it.   Only Heaven
Means *crowned*, not *vanquished*, when it says 'For-
　　given !' "
Back hurried Sister Monica ; but where
Was the poor beggar she left lying there ?
Gone ; and she searched in vain, and sought the place
For that wan woman, with the piteous face :
But only Angela at the gateway stood,
Laden with hawthorn blossoms from the wood.
And never did a day pass by again,
But the old portress, with a sigh of pain,
Would sorrow for her loitering : with a prayer
That the poor beggar, in her wild despair,
Might not have come to any ill ; and when
She ended, " God forgive her !" humbly then
Did Angela bow her head, and say " Amen !"
How pitiful her heart was ! all could trace
Something that dimmed the brightness of her face
After that day, which none had seen before ;
Not trouble—but a shadow—nothing more.

Years passed away.   Then, one dark day of dread
Saw all the sisters kneeling round a bed,
Where Angela lay dying; every breath
Struggling beneath the heavy hand of death.
But suddenly a flush lit up her cheek,
She raised her wan right hand, and strove to speak.
In sorrowing love they listened; not a sound
Or sigh disturbed the utter silence round.
The very tapers' flames were scarcely stirred,
In such hushed awe the sisters knelt and heard.
And through that silence Angela told her life:
Her sin, her flight; the sorrow and the strife,
And the return; and then clear, low and calm,
" Praise God for me, my sisters;" and the psalm
Rang up to heaven, far and clear and wide,
Again and yet again, then sank and died;
While her white face had such a smile of peace,
They saw she never heard the music cease;
And weeping sisters laid her in her tomb,
Crowned with a wreath of perfumed hawthorn bloom.

And thus the Legend ended.   It may be
Something is hidden in the mystery,
Besides the lesson of God's pardon shown,
Never enough believed, or asked, or known.
Have we not all, amid life's petty strife,
Some pure ideal of a noble life
That once seemed possible? Did we not hear
The flutter of its wings, and feel it near,
And just within our reach? It was.   And yet

We lost it in this daily jar and fret,
And now live idle in a vague regret.
But still *our place is kept*, and it will wait.
Ready for us to fill it, soon or late :
No star is ever lost we once have seen,
We always may be what we might have been.
Since Good, though only thought, has life and breath,
God's life—can always be redeemed from death ;
And evil, in its nature, is decay,
And any hour can blot it all away ;
The hopes that lost in some far distance seem,
May be the truer life, and this the dream.

ENVY.

H E was the first always : Fortune
        Shone bright in his face.
    I fought for years ; with no effort
    He conquered the place :
We ran ; my feet were all bleeding,
    But he won the race.

Spite of his many successes
    Men loved him the same ;
My one pale ray of good fortune
    Met scoffing and blame.
When we erred, they gave him pity,
    But me—only shame.

My home was still in the shadow,
   His lay in the sun :
I longed in vain : what he asked for
   It straightway was done.
Once I staked all my heart's treasure,
   We played—and he won.

Yes ; and just now I have seen him,
   Cold, smiling, and blest,
Laid in his coffin.   God help me !
   While he is at rest,
I am cursed still to live :—even
   Death loved him the best.

OVER THE MOUNTAIN.

LIKE dreary prison walls
   The stern grey mountains rise,
   Until their topmost crags
'Touch the far gloomy skies :
One steep and narrow path
   Winds up the mountain's crest,
And from our valley leads
   Out to the golden West.

I dwell here in content,
   Thankful for tranquil days ;
And yet, my eyes grow dim,
   As still I gaze and gaze

Upon that mountain pass,
  That leads—or so it seems—
To some far happy land,
  Known in a world of dreams.

And as I watch that path
  Over the distant hill,
A foolish longing comes
  My heart and soul to fill,
A painful, strange desire
  To break some weary bond,
A vague unuttered wish
  For what might lie beyond!

In that far world unknown,
  Over that distant hill,
May dwell the loved and lost,
  Lost—yet belovèd still;
I have a yearning hope,
  Half longing, and half pain,
That by that mountain pass
  They may return again.

Space may keep friends apart,
  Death has a mighty thrall;
There is another gulf
  Harder to cross than all;
Yet watching that far road,
  My heart beats full and fast—
If they should come once more,
  If they should come at last!

See, down the mountain side
  The silver vapours creep;
They hide the rocky cliffs,
  They hide the craggy steep,
They hide the narrow path
  That comes across the hill—
Oh, foolish longing, cease,
  Oh, beating Heart, be still!

BEYOND.

WE must not doubt, or fear, or dread, that love
      for life is only given,
  And that the calm and sainted dead will
  meet estranged and cold in heaven:—
Oh, Love were poor and vain indeed, based on so
  harsh and stern a creed.

True that this earth must pass away, with all the starry
      worlds of light,
With all the glory of the day, and calmer tenderness of
      night ;
For, in that radiant home can shine alone the immortal
      and divine.

Earth's lower things—her pride, her fame, her science,
      learning, wealth and power—

Slow growths that through long ages came, or fruits of
    some convulsive hour,
Whose very memory must decay—Heaven is too pure
    for such as they.

They are complete : their work is done.   So let them
    sleep in endless rest.
Love's life is only here begun, nor is, nor can be, fully
    blest ;
It has no room to spread its wings, amid this crowd
    of meaner things.

Just for the very shadow thrown upon its sweetness
    here below,
The cross that it must bear alone, and bloody baptism
    of woe,
Crowned and completed through its pain, we know
    that it shall rise again.

So if its flame burn pure and bright, here, where our
    air is dark and dense,
And nothing in this world of night lives with a living
    so intense ;
When it shall reach its home at length—how bright its
    light ! how strong its strength !

And while the vain weak loves of earth (for such base
    counterfeits abound)
Shall perish with what gave them birth—their graves
    are green and fresh around,

No funeral song shall need to rise, for the true Love
    that never dies.

If in my heart I now could fear that, risen again, we
    should not know
What was our Life of Life when here—the hearts we
    loved so much below ;
I would arise this very day, and cast so poor a thing
    away.

But Love is no such soulless clod : living, perfected it
    shall rise
Transfigured in the light of God, and giving glory to
    the skies :
And that which makes this life so sweet, shall render
    Heaven's joy complete.

A WARNING.

PLACE your hands in mine, dear,
    With their rose-leaf touch :
If you heed my warning,
    It will spare you much.

Ah ! with just such smiling
    Unbelieving eyes,
Years ago I heard it :—
    You shall be more wise.

You have one great treasure,
  Joy for all your life ;
Do not let it perish
  In one reckless strife.

Do not venture all, child,
  In one frail, weak heart ;
So, through any shipwreck,
  You may save a part.

Where your soul is tempted
  Most to trust your fate,
There, with double caution,
  Linger, fear, and wait

Measure all you give—still
  Counting what you take ;
Love for love : so placing
  Each an equal stake.

Treasure love ; though ready
  Still to live without.
In your fondest trust, keep
  Just one thread of doubt.

Build on no to-morrow ;
  Love has but to-day :
If the links seem slackening,
  Cut the bond away.

Trust no prayer nor promise ;
  Words are grains of sand :

To keep your heart unbroken,
  Hold it in your hand.

That your love may finish
  Calm as it begun,
Learn this lesson better,
  Dear, than I have done.

Years hence, perhaps, this warning
  You shall give again,
In just the self-same words, dear,
  And—just as much—in vain.

MAXIMUS.

MANY, if God should make them kings,
  Might not disgrace the throne He
    gave ;
How few who could as well fulfil
  The holier office of a slave.

I hold him great who, for Love's sake,
  Can give, with generous, earnest will,—
Yet he who takes for Love's sweet sake,
  I think I hold more generous still.

I prize the instinct that can turn
  From vain pretence with proud disdain ;
Yet more I prize a simple heart
  Paying credulity with pain.

I bow before the noble mind
    That freely some great wrong forgives;
Yet nobler is the one forgiven,
    Who bears that burden well, and lives.

It may be hard to gain, and still
    To keep a lowly steadfast heart;
Yet he who loses has to fill
    A harder and a truer part.

Glorious it is to wear the crown
    Of a deserved and pure success;—
He who knows how to fail has won
    A Crown whose lustre is not less.

Great may he be who can command
    And rule with just and tender sway;
Yet is diviner wisdom taught
    Better by him who can obey.

Blessèd are those who die for God,
    And earn the Martyr's crown of light—
Yet he who lives for God may be
    A greater Conqueror in His sight.

OPTIMUS.

THERE is a deep and subtle snare
   Whose sure temptation hardly fails,
   Which, just because it looks so fair,
Only a noble heart assails.

So all the more we need be strong
Against this false and seeming Right ;
Which none the less is deadly wrong,
Because it glitters clothed in light.

When duties unfulfilled remain,
Or noble works are left unplanned,
Or when great deeds cry out in vain
On coward heart and trembling hand,—

Then will a seeming Angel speak :—
" The hours are fleeting—great the need—
If thou art strong and others weak,
Thine be the effort and the deed.

" Deaf are their ears who ought to hear ;
Idle their hands, and dull their soul ;
While sloth, or ignorance, or fear,
Fetters them with a blind control.

Q

" Sort thou the tangled web aright ;
Take thou the toil—take thou the pain :
For fear the hour begin its flight,
While Right and Duty plead in vain."

And now it is I bid thee pause,
Nor let this Tempter bend thy will :
There are diviner, truer laws
That teach a nobler lesson still.

Learn that each duty makes its claim
Upon one soul: not each on all.
How, if God speaks thy Brother's name,
Dare thou make answer to the call ?

The greater peril in the strife,
The less this evil should be done ;
For as in battle, so in life,
Danger and honour still are one.

Arouse him then :—this is thy part :
Show him the claim ; point out the need ;
And nerve his arm, and cheer his heart ;
Then stand aside, and say " God speed ! "

Smooth thou his path ere it is trod ;
Burnish the arms that he must wield ;
And pray, with all thy strength, that God
May crown him Victor of the field.

And then, I think, thy soul shall feel
A nobler thrill of true content,

Than if presumptuous, eager zeal
Had seized a crown for others meant.

And even that very deed shall shine
In mystic sense, divine and true,
More wholly and more purely thine—
Because it is another's too.

A LOST CHORD.

SEATED one day at the Organ,
     I was weary and ill at ease,
     And my fingers wandered idly
Over the noisy keys.

I do not know what I was playing,
     Or what I was dreaming then;
But I struck one chord of music,
     Like the sound of a great Amen.

It flooded the crimson twilight
     Like the close of an Angel's Psalm,
And it lay on my fevered spirit
     With a touch of infinite calm.

It quieted pain and sorrow,
     Like love overcoming strife;
It seemed the harmonious echo
     From our discordant life.

It linked all perplexèd meanings
Into one perfect peace,
And trembled away into silence
As if it were loth to cease.

I have sought, but I seek it vainly,
That one lost chord divine,
Which came from the soul of the Organ,
And entered into mine.

It may be that Death's bright angel
Will speak in that chord again,—
It may be that only in Heaven
I shall hear that grand Amen.

TOO LATE.

HUSH ! speak low ; tread softly ;
Draw the sheet aside ;—
Yes, she does look peaceful ;
With that smile she died.

Yet stern want and sorrow
Even now you trace
On the wan, worn features
Of the still white face.

Restless, helpless, hopeless,
  Was her bitter part ;—
Now—how still the Violets
  Lie upon her Heart ;

She who toiled and laboured
  For her daily bread ;
See the velvet hangings
  Of this stately bed.

Yes, they did forgive her ;
  Brought her home at last ;
Strove to cover over
  Their relentless past.

Ah, they would have given
  Wealth, and home, and pride,
To see her just look happy
  Once before she died !

They strove hard to please her,
  But, when death is near,
All you know is deadened,
  Hope, and joy, and fear.

And besides, one sorrow
  Deeper still—one pain
Was beyond them : healing
  Came to-day—in vain !

If she had but lingered
　Just a few hours more ;
Or had this letter reached her
　Just one day before !

I can almost pity
　Even him to-day ;
Though he let this anguish
　Eat her heart away.

Yet she never blamed him :—
　One day you shall know
How this sorrow happened ;
　It was long ago.

I have read the letter :
　Many a weary year,
For one word she hungered—
　There are thousands here.

If she could but hear it,
　Could but understand ;
See—I put the letter
　In her cold white hand.

Even these words, so longed for,
　Do not stir her rest ;
Well—I should not murmur,
　For God judges best.

She needs no more pity,—
But I mourn his fate,
When he hears his letter
Came a day too late.

THE REQUITAL.

LOUD roared the Tempest,
    Fast fell the sleet;
A little Child Angel
Passed down the street,
With trailing pinions,
    And weary feet.

The moon was hidden ;
    No stars were bright ;
So she could not shelter
    In heaven that night,
For the Angels' ladders
    Are rays of light.

She beat her wings
    At each window pane,
And pleaded for shelter,
    But all in vain :—
" Listen," they said,
    " To the pelting rain ! "

She sobbed, as the laughter
  And mirth grew higher,
" Give me rest and shelter
  Beside your fire,
And I will give you
  Your heart's desire."

The dreamer sat watching
  His embers gleam,
While his heart was floating
  Down hope's bright stream ;
. . . So he wove her wailing
  Into his dream.

The worker toiled on,
  For his time was brief ;
The mourner was nursing
  Her own pale grief :
They heard not the promise
  That brought relief.

But fiercer the Tempest
  Rose than before,
When the Angel paused
  At a humble door,
And asked for shelter
  And help once more.

A weary woman,
  Pale, worn, and thin,
With the brand upon her
  Of want and sin,

Heard the Child Angel
  And took her in.

Took her in gently,
  And did her best
To dry her pinions;
  And made her rest
With tender pity
  Upon her breast.

When the eastern morning
  Grew bright and red,
Up the first sunbeam
  The Angel fled;
Having kissed the woman
  And left her—dead

RETURNED—"MISSING."

(FIVE YEARS AFTER.)

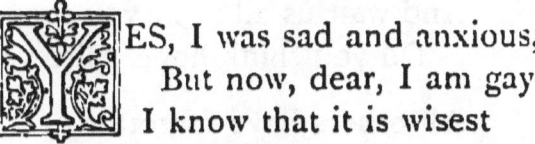 ES, I was sad and anxious,
  But now, dear, I am gay;
  I know that it is wisest
To put all hope away:—
Thank God that I have done so
And can be calm to-day.

For hope deferred—you know it,
 Once made my heart so sick :
Now, I expect no longer ;
 It is but the old trick
Of hope, that makes me tremble,
 And makes my heart beat quick.

All day I sit here calmly ;
 Not as I did before,
Watching for one whose footstep
 Comes never, never more. . . .
Hush ! was that some one passing,
 Who paused beside the door ?

For years I hung on chances,
 Longing for just one word ;
At last I feel it :—silence
 Will never more be stirred. . . .
Tell me once more that rumour,
 You fancied you had heard.

Life has more things to dwell on
 Than just one useless pain,
Useless and past for ever ;
 But noble things remain,
And wait us all : . . . you too, dear.
 Do you think hope quite vain ?

All others have forgotten,
 'Tis right I should forget,
Nor live on a keen longing
 Which shadows forth regret :

Are not the letters coming ?
   The sun is almost set.

Now that my restless legion
   Of hopes and fears is fled,
Reading is joy and comfort
   . . . This very day I read,
Oh, such a strange returning
   Of one whom all thought dead !

Not that *I* dream or fancy,
   You know all that is past ;
Earth has no hope to give me,
   And yet :—Time flies so fast
That all but the impossible
   Might be brought back at last.

IN THE WOOD.

IN the wood where shadows are deepest
   From the branches overhead,
Where the wild wood-strawberries
     cluster,
 And the softest moss is spread,
I met to-day with a fairy,
   And I followed her where she led.

Some magical words she uttered,
  I alone could understand,
For the sky grew bluer and brighter;
  While there rose on either hand
The cloudy walls of a palace
  That was built in Fairy-land.

And I stood in a strange enchantment;
  I had known it all before :
In my heart of hearts was the magic
  Of days that will come no more,
The magic of joy departed,
  That Time can never restore.

That never, ah, never, never,
  Never again can be :—
Shall I tell you what powerful fairy
  Built up this palace for me?
It was only a little white Violet
  I found at the root of a tree.

TWO WORLDS.

GOD'S world is bathed in beauty,
    God's world is steeped in light ;
  It is the self-same glory
  That makes the day so bright,
Which thrills the earth with music,
  Or hangs the stars in night.

Hid in earth's mines of silver,
   Floating on clouds above,—
Ringing in Autumn's tempest.
   Murmured by every dove ;
One thought fills God's creation—
   His own great name of Love !

In God's world Strength is lovely.
   And so is Beauty strong,
And Light—God's glorious shadow—
   To both great gifts belong ;
And they all melt into sweetness,
   And fill the earth with Song.

Above God's world bends Heaven.
   With day's kiss pure and bright,
Or folds her still more fondly
   In the tender shade of night ;
And she casts back Heaven's sweetness.
   In fragrant love and light.

God's world has one great echo ;
   Whether calm blue mists are curled,
Or lingering dew-drops quiver,
   Or red storms are unfurled ;
The same deep love is throbbing
   Through the great heart of God's world

Man's world is black and blighted,
   Steeped through with self and sin ;

And should his feeble purpose
  Some feeble good begin,
The work is marred and tainted
  By Leprosy within.

Man's world is bleak and bitter;
  Wherever he has trod
He spoils the tender beauty
  That blossoms on the sod,
And blasts the loving Heaven
  Of the great, good world of God.

There Strength on coward weakness
  In cruel might will roll;
Beauty and Joy are cankers
  That eat away the soul;
And Love—Oh God, avenge it—
  The plague-spot of the whole.

Man's world is Pain and Terror;
  He found it pure and fair,
And wove in nets of sorrow
  The golden summer air.
Black, hideous, cold, and dreary,
  Man's curse, not God's, is there.

And yet God's world is speaking:
  Man will not hear it call;
But listens where the echoes
  Of his own discords fall.

Then clamours back to Heaven
  That God has done it all.

Oh God, man's heart is darkened,
  He will not understand !
Show him Thy cloud and fire ;
  And, with Thine own right hand
Then lead him through his desert,
  Back to Thy Holy Land !

A NEW MOTHER.

 WAS with my lady when she died :
I it was who guided her weak hand
  For a blessing on each little head,
Laid her baby by her on the bed,
Heard the words they could not understand.

And I drew them round my knee that night,
Hushed their childish glee, and made them say
  They would keep her words with loving tears,
  They would not forget her dying fears
Lest the thought of her should fade away.

I, who guessed what her last dread had been,
Made a promise to that still, cold face,

That her children's hearts, at any cost,
Should be with the mother they had lost,
When a stranger came to take her place.

And I knew so much ! for I had lived
With my lady since her childhood : known
  What her young and happy days had been,
  And the grief no other eyes had seen
I had watched and sorrowed for alone.

Ah ! she once had such a happy smile !
I had known how sorely she was tried :
  Six short years before, her eyes were bright
  As her little blue-eyed May's that night,
When she stood by her dead mother's side.

No—I will not say he was unkind ;
But she had been used to love and praise.
  He was somewhat grave—perhaps, in truth,
  Could not weave her joyous, smiling youth,
Into all his stern and serious ways.

She, who should have reigned a blooming flower,
First in pride and honour, as in grace,—
  She, whose will had once ruled all around,
  Queen and darling of us all—she found
Change indeed in that cold, stately place.

Yet she would not blame him, even to me,
Though she often sat and wept alone ;

But she could not hide it near her death,
When she said with her last struggling breath,
  " Let my babies still remain my own ! "

I it was who drew the sheet aside,
When he saw his dead wife's face.   That test
    Seemed to strike right to his heart.   He said,
    In a strange, low whisper, to the dead,
" God knows, love, I did it for the best ! "

And he wept—Oh yes, I will be just—
When I brought the children to him there—
    Wondering sorrow in their baby eyes ;
    And he soothed them with his fond replies,
Bidding me give double love and care.

Ah, I loved them well for her dear sake :
Little Arthur, with his serious air ;
    May, with all her mother's pretty ways,
    Blushing, and at any word of praise
Shaking out her sunny golden hair.

And the little one of all—poor child !
She had cost that dear and precious life.
    Once Sir Arthur spoke my lady's name,
    When the baby's gloomy christening came,
And he called her " Olga—like my wife ! "

Save that time, he never spoke of her :
He grew graver, sterner every day ;

R

And the children felt it, for they dropped
Low their voices, and their laughter stopped
While he stood and watched them at their play.

No, he never named their mother's name.
But I told them of her: told them all
　　She had been; so gentle, good, and bright;
　　And I always took them every night
Where her picture hung in the great hall.

There she stood: white daisies in her hand,
And her red lips parted as to speak
　　With a smile; the blue and sunny air
　　Seemed to stir her floating golden hair,
And to bring a faint blush on her cheek.

Well, so time passed on; a year was gone,
And Sir Arthur had been much away.
　　Then the news came! I shed many tears
　　When I saw the truth of all my fears
Rise before me on that bitter day.

Any one but her I could have borne!
But my lady loved her as her friend.
　　Through their childhood and their early youth,
　　How she used to count upon the truth
Of this friendship that would never end!

Older, graver than my lady was,
Whose young, gentle heart on her relied

She would give advice, and praise, and blame,
And my lady leant on Margaret's name,
   As her dearest comfort, help, and guide.

I had never liked her, and I think
That my lady grew to doubt her too,
   Since her marriage; for she named her less,
   Never saw her, and I used to guess
At some secret wrong I never knew.

That might be or not.   But now, to hear
She would come and reign here in her stead,
   With the pomp and splendour of a bride:
   Would no thought reproach her in her pride
With the silent memory of the dead?

So, the day came, and the bells rang out,
And I laid the children's black aside;
   And I held each little trembling hand,
   As I strove to make them understand
They must greet their father's new-made bride.

Ah, Sir Arthur might look grave and stern,
And his lady's eyes might well grow dim,
   When the children shrank in fear away,—
   Little Arthur hid his face, and May
Would not raise her eyes, or speak to him.

When Sir Arthur bade them greet their " mother,"
I was forced to chide, yet proud to hear

How my little loving May replied,
With her mother's pretty air of pride,—
"Our dear mother has been dead a year!"

Ah, the lady's tears might well fall fast,
As she kissed them, and then turned away.
  She might strive to smile or to forget,
  But I think some shadow of regret
Must have risen to blight her wedding-day.

She had some strange touch of self-reproach ;
For she used to linger day by day,
  By the nursery door, or garden gate,
  With a sad, calm, wistful look, and wait
Watching the three children at their play.

But they always shrank away from her
When she strove to comfort their alarms,
  And their grave, cold silence to beguile :
  Even little Olga's baby-smile
Quivered into tears when in her arms.

I could never chide them : for I saw
How their mother's memory grew more deep
  In their hearts.   Each night I had to tell
  Stories of her whom I loved so well
When a child, to send them off to sleep.

But Sir Arthur—Oh, this was too hard !—
He, who had been always stern and sad

In my lady's time, seemed to rejoice
Each day more ; and I could hear his voice
Even, sounding younger and more glad.

He might perhaps have blamed them, but his wife
Never failed to take the children's part :
She would stay him with her pleading tone,
Saying she would strive, and strive alone,
Till she gained each little wayward heart.

And she strove indeed, and seemed to be
Always waiting for their love, in vain ;
Yet, when May had most her mother's look,
Then the lady's calm, cold accents shook
With some memory of reproachful pain.

Little May would never call her Mother :
So, one day, the lady, bending low,
Kissed her golden curls, and softly said,
" Sweet one, call me Margaret, instead,—
Your dear mother used to call me so."

She was gentle, kind, and patient too,
Yet in vain : the children held apart.
Ah, their mother's gentle memory dwelt
Near them, and her little orphans felt
She had the first claim upon their heart.

So three years passed ; then the war broke out ;
And a rumour seemed to spread and rise ;

First we guessed what sorrow must befall,
Then all doubt fled, for we read it all
In the depths of her despairing eyes.

Yes ; Sir Arthur had been called away
To that scene of slaughter, fear, and strife,—
    Now he seemed to know with double pain,
    The cold, bitter gulf that must remain
To divide his children from his wife.

Nearer came the day he was to sail,
Deeper grew the coming woe and fear,
    When, one night, the children at my knee
    Knelt to say their evening prayer to me,
I looked up and saw Sir Arthur near.

There they knelt with folded hands, and said
Low, soft words in stammering accents sweet ;
    In the firelight shone their golden hair
    And white robes : my darlings looked so fair,
With their little bare and rosy feet !

There he waited till their low " Amen ; "
Stopped the rosy lips raised for " Good night ! "—
    Drew them with a fond clasp, close and near,
    As he bade them stay with him, and hear
Something that would make his heart more light.

Little Olga crept into his arms ;
Arthur leant upon his shoulder ; May

Knelt beside him, with her earnest eyes
Lifted up in patient, calm surprise—
  I can almost hear his words to-day.

"Years ago, my children, years ago,
When your mother was a child, she came
  From her northern home, and here she met
  Love for love, and comfort for regret,
In one early friend,—you know her name.

"And this friend—a few years older—gave
Such fond care, such love, that day by day
  The new home grew happy, joy complete,
  Studies easier, and play more sweet,
While all childish sorrows passed away.

"And your mother—fragile, like my May—
Leant on this deep love,—nor leant in vain.
  For this friend (strong, generous, noble heart!)
  Gave the sweet, and took the bitter part,—
Brought her all the joy, and kept the pain.

"Years passed on, and then I saw them first :
It was hard to say which was most fair,
  Your sweet mother's bright and blushing face,
  Or the graver Margaret's stately grace ;
Golden locks, or braided raven hair.

"Then it happened, by a strange, sad fate,
One thought entered into each young soul :

Joy for one—if for the other pain;
Loss for one—if for the other gain:
One must lose, and one possess the whole.

" And so this—this—what they cared for—came
And belonged to Margaret: was her own.
　　But she laid the gift aside, to take
　　Pain and sorrow for your mother's sake,
And none knew it but herself alone.

" Then she travelled far away, and none
The strange mystery of her absence knew.
　　Margaret's secret thought was never told:
　　Even your mother thought her changed and cold,
And for many years I thought so too.

" She was gone; and then your mother took
That poor gift which Margaret laid aside:
　　Flower, or toy, or trinket, matters not:
　　What it was had better be forgot . . .
It was just then she became my bride.

" Now, I think May knows the hope I have.
Arthur, darling, can you guess the rest?
　　Even my little Olga understands
　　Great gifts can be given by little hands,
Since of all gifts Love is still the best.

" Margaret is my dear and honoured wife,
And I hold her so.   But she can claim

From your hearts, dear ones, a loving debt
I can neither pay, nor yet forget:
You can give it in your mother's name.

" Earth spoils even Love, and here a shade
On the purest, noblest heart may fall :
　　Now your mother dwells in perfect light,
　　She will bless us, I believe, to-night,—
She is happy now, and she knows all."

Next day was farewell—a day of tears ;
Yet Sir Arthur, as he rode away,
　　And turned back to see his lady stand
　　With the children clinging to her hand,
Looked as if it were a happy day.

Ah, they loved her soon ! The little one
Crept into her arms as to a nest ;
　　Arthur always with her now ; and May
　　Growing nearer to her every day :—
—Well, I loved my own dear lady best.

GIVE PLACE.

STARRY Crowns of Heaven
　　Set in azure night !
　Linger yet a little
Ere you hide your light :—
　　—Nay ; let Starlight fade away
　Heralding the day !

Snowflakes pure and spotless,
  Still, oh, still remain,
Binding dreary winter,
  In your silver chain :—
    —Nay; but melt at once and bring
    Radiant sunny Spring !

Blossoms, gentle blossoms,
  Do not wither yet ;
Still for you the sun shines,
  Still the dews are wet :—
    —Nay; but fade and wither fast,
    Fruit must come at last !

Joy, so true and tender,
  Dare you not abide?
Will you spread your pinions,
  Must you leave our side ?
    —Nay; an Angel's shining grace
    Waits to fill your place !

MY WILL.

SINCE I have no lands or houses,
  And no hoarded golden store,
  What can I leave those who love me
When they see my face no more ?

Do not smile; I am not jesting,
  Though my words sound gay and light,
Listen to me, dearest Alice,
  I will make my Will to-night.

First for Mabel,—who will never
  Let the dust of future years
Dim the thought of me, but keep it
  Brighter still : perhaps with tears.
In whose eyes, whate'er I glance at,
  Touch, or praise, will always shine,
Through a strange and sacred radiance,
  By Love's Charter, wholly mine ;
She will never lend to others
  Slenderest link of thought I claim,
I will, therefore, to her keeping
  Leave my memory and my name.

Bertha will do truer service
  To her kind than I have done,
So I leave to her young spirit
  The long Work I have begun.
Well ! the threads are tangled, broken,
  And the colours do not blend,
She will bend her earnest striving
  Both to finish and amend :
And, when it is all completed,
  Strong with care and rich with skill,
Just because my hands began it,
  She will love it better still.

Ruth shall have my dearest token,
　The one link I dread to break,
The one duty that I live for,
　She, when I am gone, will take.
Sacred is the trust I leave her,
　Needing patience, prayer, and tears;
I have striven to fulfil it,
　As she knows—these many years.
Sometimes hopeless, faint, and weary,
　Yet a blessing shall remain
With the task, and Ruth will prize it
　For my many hours of pain.

What must I leave you, my Alice?
　Nothing, Love, to do or bear,
Nothing that can dim your blue eyes
　With the slightest cloud of care.
I will leave my heart to love you,
　With the tender faith of old;
Still to comfort, warm, and light you,
　Should your life grow dark or cold.
No one else, my child, can claim it;
　Though you find old scars of pain,
They were only wounds, my darling,
　There is not, I trust, one stain.

Are my gifts indeed so worthless
　Now the slender sum is told?
Well, I know not: years may bless them
　With a nobler price than gold.

My Will.

Am I poor? ah no, most wealthy,
　　Not in these poor gifts you take,
But in the true hearts that tell me
　　You will keep them for my sake.

KING AND SLAVE.

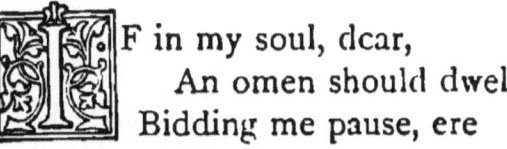F in my soul, dear,
　　An omen should dwell,
　　Bidding me pause, ere
　　I love thee too well ;
If the whole circle,
　　Of noble and wise,
With stern forebodings,
　　Between us should rise.

I will tell *them*, dear,
　　That Love reigns—a King,
Where storms cannot reach him,
　　And words cannot sting ;
He counts it dishonour
　　His faith to recall ;
He trusts ;—and for ever
　　He gives—and gives all !

I will tell *thee*, dear,
　　That Love is—a Slave,

Who dreads thought of freedom,
    As life dreads the grave ;
And if doubt or peril
    Of change there may be,
Such fear would but drive him
    Still nearer to thee !

A CHANT.

"*Benedictus qui venit in nomine Domini.*"

I.

WHO is the Angel that cometh ?
                Life !
Let us not question what he brings,
        Peace or Strife,
Under the shade of his mighty wings,
            One by one,
        Are his secrets told ;
            One by one,
Lit by the rays of each morning sun,
    Shall a new flower its petals unfold,
    With the mystery hid in its heart of gold.
We will arise and go forth to greet him,
    Singing, gladly, with one accord ;—
" Blessed is he that cometh
        In the name of the Lord ! "

II.

Who is the Angel that cometh?
   Joy!
Look at his glittering rainbow wings—
   No alloy
Lies in the radiant gifts he brings;
    Tender and sweet,
    He is come to-day,
    Tender and sweet:
While chains of love on his silver feet
 Will hold him in lingering fond delay.
 But greet him quickly, he will not stay,
Soon he will leave us; but though for others
 All his brightest treasures are stored;—
" Blessed is he that cometh
  In the name of the Lord!"

III.

Who is the Angel that cometh?
   Pain!
Let us arise and go forth to greet him :
   Not in vain
Is the summons come for us to meet him;
    He will stay,
   And darken our sun;
    He will stay
A desolate night, a weary day.
 Since in that shadow our work is done,
 And in that shadow our crowns are won,

Let us say still, while his bitter chalice
  Slowly into our hearts is poured,—
"Blessed is he that cometh
  In the name of the Lord!"

IV.

Who is the Angel that cometh?
    Death!
But do not shudder and do not fear;
    Hold your breath,
For a kingly presence is drawing near.
    Cold and bright
  Is his flashing steel,
    Cold and bright
The smile that comes like a starry light
  To calm the terror and grief we feel;
  He comes to help and to save and heal:
Then let us, baring our hearts and kneeling,
  Sing, while we wait this Angel's sword.—
"Blessed is he that cometh
  In the name of the Lord!"

DREAM-LIFE.

LISTEN, friend, and I will tell you
    Why I sometimes seem so glad,
  Then, without a reason changing,
Soon become so grave and sad.

Half my life I live a beggar,
  Ragged, helpless, and alone ;
But the other half a monarch,
  With my courtiers round my throne.

Half my life is full of sorrow,
  Half of joy, still fresh and new ;
One of these lives is a fancy,
  But the other one is true.

While I live and feast on gladness,
  Still I feel the thought remain,
This must soon end,—nearer, nearer,
  Comes the life of grief and pain.

While I live a wretched beggar,
  One bright hope my lot can cheer ;
Soon, soon, thou shalt have thy kingdom,
  Brighter hours are drawing near.

So you see my life is twofold,
  Half a pleasure, half a grief ;
Thus all joy is somewhat tempered.
  And all sorrow finds relief.

Which, you ask me, is the real life,
  Which the Dream—the joy, or woe?
Hush, friend ! it is little matter,
  And, indeed—I never know.

S

REST.

SPREAD, spread thy silver wings, oh Dove!
    And seek for rest by land and sea,
    And bring the tidings back to me
For thee and me and those I love.
    Look how my Dove soars far away;
    Go with her, heart of mine, I pray;
    Go where her fluttering silver pinions
    Follow the track of the crimson day.

Is rest where cloudlets slowly creep,
And sobbing winds forget to grieve,
And quiet waters gently heave,
As if they rocked the ship to sleep?
    Ah no! that southern vapour white
    Will bring a tempest ere the night,
    And thunder through the quiet Heaven,
    Lashing the sea in its angry might.

The battle-field lies still and cold,
While stars that watch in silent light
Gleam here and there on weapons bright,
In weary sleepers' slackened hold;
    Nay, though they dream of no alarm,
    One bugle sound will stir that calm,
    And all the strength of two great nations,
    Eager for battle, will rise and arm.

Pause where the Pilgrims' day is done,
Where scrip and staff aside are laid,
And, resting in the silent shade,
They watch the slowly sinking sun.
> Ah no ! that worn and weary band
> Must journey long before they stand,
> With bleeding feet, and hearts rejoicing,
> Kissing the dust of the Holy Land.

Then find a soul who meets at last
A noble prize but hard to gain,
Or joy long pleaded for in vain,
Now sweeter for a bitter past.
> Ah no ! for Time can rob her yet,
> And even should cruel Time forget,
> Then Death will come, and, unrelenting,
> Brand her with sorrowful long regret.

Seek farther, farther yet, oh Dove !
Beyond the Land, beyond the Sea,
There shall be rest for thee and me,
For thee and me and those I love.
> I heard a promise gently fall,
> I heard a far-off Shepherd call
> The weary and the broken-hearted,
> Promising rest unto each and all.

It is not marred by outward strife,
It is not lost in calm repose,
It heedeth neither joys nor woes,
Is not disturbed by death or life ;

Through, and beyond them, lies our Rest :
Then cease, oh Heart, thy longing quest !
And thou, my Dove, with silver pinions
Flutter again to thy quiet nest !

THE TYRANT AND THE CAPTIVE.

IT was midnight when I listened,
    And I heard two Voices speak ;
    One was harsh, and stern, and cruel,
And the other soft and weak :
Yet I saw no Vision enter,
    And I heard no steps depart,
Of this Tyrant and his Captive, . .
    Fate it might be and a *Heart.*

Thus the stern Voice spake in triumph :—
    "I have shut your life away
From the radiant world of nature,
    And the perfumed light of day.
You, who loved to steep your spirit
    In the charm of Earth's delight,
See no glory of the daytime,
    And no sweetness of the night."

But the soft Voice answered calmly :
    "Nay, for when the March winds bring

Just a whisper to my window,
   I can dream the rest of Spring;
And to-day I saw a Swallow
   Flitting past my prison bars,
And my cell has just one corner
   Whence at night I see the stars."

But its bitter taunt repeating,
   Cried the harsh Voice:—"Where are they—
All the friends of former hours,
   Who forget your name to-day?
All the links of love are shattered,
   Which you thought so strong before;
And your very heart is lonely,
   And alone since loved no more."

But the low Voice spoke still lower :—
   " Nay, I know the golden chain
Of my love is purer, stronger,
   For the cruel fire of pain :
They remember me no longer,
   But I, grieving here alone,
Bind their souls to me for ever
   By the love within their own."

But the Voice cried:—" Once remember
   You devoted soul and mind
To the welfare of your brethren,
   And the service of your kind.
Now, what sorrow can you comfort ?
   You, who lie in helpless pain,

With an impotent compassion
  Fretting out your life in vain."

" Nay ;" and then the gentle answer
  Rose more loud, and full, and clear :
" For the sake of all my brethren
  I thank God that I am here !
Poor had been my Life's best efforts,
  Now I waste no thought or breath—
For the prayer of those who suffer
  Has the strength of Love and Death."

THE CARVER'S LESSON.

TRUST me, no mere skill of subtle tracery,
  No mere practice of a dexterous hand,
  Will suffice, without a hidden spirit,
That we may, or may not, understand.

And those quaint old fragments that are left us
  Have their power in this,—the Carver brought
Earnest care, and reverent patience, only
  Worthily to clothe some noble thought.

Shut then in the petals of the flowers,
  Round the stems of all the lilies twine,
Hide beneath each bird's or angel's pinion,
  Some wise meaning or some thought divine.

Place in stony hands that pray for ever
 Tender words of peace, and strive to wind
Round the leafy scrolls and fretted niches
 Some true, loving message to your kind.

Some will praise, some blame, and, soon forgetting,
 Come and go, nor even pause to gaze ;
Only now and then a passing stranger
 Just may loiter with a word of praise.

But I think, when years have floated onward,
 And the stone is grey, and dim, and old,
And the hand forgotten that has carved it,
 And the heart that dreamt it still and cold ;

There may come some weary soul, o'erladen
 With perplexèd struggle in his brain,
Or, it may be, fretted with life's turmoil,
 Or made sore with some perpetual pain.

Then, I think those stony hands will open,
 And the gentle lilies overflow,
With the blessing and the loving token
 That you hid there many years ago.

And the tendrils will unroll, and teach him
 How to solve the problem of his pain ;
And the birds' and angels' wings shake downward
 On his heart a sweet and tender rain.

While he marvels at his fancy, reading
   Meaning in that quaint and ancient scroll,
Little guessing that the loving Carver
   Left a message for his weary soul.

THREE ROSES.

JUST when the red June Roses blow
   She gave me one,—a year ago.
   A Rose whose crimson breath revealed
The secret that its heart concealed,
And whose half shy, half tender grace
Blushed back upon the giver's face.
   A year ago—a year ago—
   To hope was not to know.

Just when the red June Roses blow
I plucked her one,—a month ago :
Its half-blown crimson to eclipse,
I laid it on her smiling lips ;
The balmy fragrance of the south
Drew sweetness from her sweeter mouth.
   Swiftly do golden hours creep,—
   To hold is not to keep.

The red June Roses now are past,
This very day I broke the last—

And now its perfumed breath is hid,
With her, beneath a coffin-lid ;
There will its petals fall apart,
And wither on her icy heart :—
   At three red Roses' cost
   My world was gained and lost.

MY PICTURE GALLERY.

I.

YOU write and think of me, my friend, with
      pity ;
  While you are basking in the light of Rome,
Shut up within the heart of this great city,
Too busy and too poor to leave my home.

II.

You think my life debarred all rest or pleasure,
Chained all day to my ledger and my pen ;
Too sickly even to use my little leisure
To bear me from the strife and din of men.

III.

Well, it is true ; yet, now the days are longer,
At sunset I can lay my writing down,
And slowly crawl (summer has made me stronger)
Just to the nearest outskirt of the town.

IV.

There a wide Common, blackened though and dreary
With factory smoke, spreads outward to the West ;
I lie down on the parched-up grass, if weary,
Or lean against a broken wall to rest.

V.

So might a King, turning to Art's rich treasure,
At evening, when the cares of state were done,
Enter his royal gallery, drinking pleasure
Slowly from each great picture, one by one.

VI.

Towards the West I turn my weary spirit,
And watch my pictures : one each night is mine.
Earth and my soul, sick of day's toil, inherit
A portion of that luminous peace divine.

VII.

There I have seen a sunset's crimson glory,
Burn as if earth were one great Altar's blaze ;
Or, like the closing of a piteous story,
Light up the misty world with dying rays.

VIII.

There I have seen the Clouds, in pomp and splendour,
Their gold and purple banners all unfurl ;
There I have watched colours, more faint and tender
Than pure and delicate tints upon a pearl.

IX.

Skies strewn with roses fading, fading slowly,
While one star trembling watched the daylight die;
Or deep in gloom a sunset, hidden wholly,
Save through gold rents torn in a violet sky.

X.

Or parted clouds, as if asunder riven
By some great angel—and beyond a space
Of far-off tranquil light; the gates of Heaven
Will lead us grandly to as calm a place.

XI.

Or stern dark walls of cloudy mountain ranges
Hid all the wonders that we knew must be;
While, far on high, some little white clouds' changes
Revealed the glory they alone could see.

XII.

Or in wild wrath the affrighted clouds lay shattered,
Like treasures of the lost Hesperides,
All in a wealth of ruined splendour scattered,
Save one strange light on distant silver seas.

XIII.

What land or time can claim the Master Painter,
Whose art could teach him half such gorgeous dyes?
Or skill so rare, but purer hues and fainter
Melt every evening in my western skies.

XIV

So there I wait, until the shade has lengthened,
And night's blue misty curtain floated down ;
Then, with my heart calmed, and my spirit strengthened,
I crawl once more back to the sultry town.

XV.

What Monarch, then, has nobler recreations
Than mine? Or where the great and classic Land
Whose wealth of Art delights the gathered nations
That owns a Picture Gallery half as grand?

SENT TO HEAVEN.

 HAD a Message to send her,
　　To her whom my soul loved best ;
But I had my task to finish,
And she was gone home to rest.

To rest in the far bright heaven :
　　Oh, so far away from here,
It was vain to speak to my darling,
　　For I knew she could not hear !

I had a message to send her,
　　So tender, and true, and sweet,
I longed for an Angel to bear it,
　　And lay it down at her feet.

I placed it, one summer evening,
   On a Cloudlet's fleecy breast ;
But it faded in golden splendour,
   And died in the crimson west.

I gave it the Lark next morning,
   And I watched it soar and soar;
But its pinions grew faint and weary,
   And it fluttered to earth once more.

To the heart of a Rose I told it :
   And the perfume, sweet and rare,
Growing faint on the blue bright ether,
   Was lost in the balmy air.

I laid it upon a Censer,
   And I saw the incense rise ;
But its clouds of rolling silver
   Could not reach the far blue skies.

I cried, in my passionate longing :—
   " Has the Earth no Angel-friend
Who will carry my love the message
   That my heart desires to send ? "

Then I heard a strain of music,
   So mighty, so pure, so clear,
That my very sorrow was silent,
   And my heart stood still to hear.

And I felt, in my soul's deep yearning,
　At last the sure answer stir :—
" The music will go up to Heaven,
　And carry my thought to her."

It rose in harmonious rushing
　Of mingled voices and strings,
And I tenderly laid my message
　On the Music's outspread wings.

I heard it float farther and farther,
　In sound more perfect than speech :
Farther than sight can follow,
　Farther than soul can reach.

And I know that at last my message
　Has passed through the golden gate :
So my heart is no longer restless,
　And I am content to wait.

NEVER AGAIN.

NEVER again ! " vow hearts when reunited,
　" Never again shall Love be cast aside !
　For ever now the shadow has departed !
Nor bitter sorrow, veiled in scornful pride,
Shall feign indifference, or affect disdain,—
Never, oh Love, again, never again ! "

" Never again ! " so sobs, in broken accents,
　　A soul laid prostrate at a holy shrine,—
" Once more, once more forgive, oh Lord, and pardon,
　　My wayward life shall bend to love divine ;
And never more shall sin its whiteness stain,—
Never, oh God, again, never again ! "

" Never again ! " so speaketh one forsaken,
　　In the blank desolate passion of despair,—
" Never again shall the bright dream I cherished
　　Delude my heart, for bitter truth is there,—
The angel, Hope, shall still thy cruel pain
Never again, my heart, never again ! "

" Never again ! " so speaks the sudden silence,
　　When round the hearth gathers each well-known
　　　　face,—
But one is missing, and no future presence,
　　However dear, can fill that vacant place ;
For ever shall the burning thought remain,—
" Never, beloved, again ! never again ! "

" Never again ! " so—but beyond our hearing—
　　Ring out far voices fading up the sky ;
Never again shall earthly care and sorrow
　　Weigh down the wings that bear those souls on high ;
Listen, oh earth, and hear that glorious strain,—
" Never, never again ! never again ! "

LISTENING ANGELS.

BLUE against the bluer Heavens
    Stood the mountain, calm and still,
  Two white Angels, bending earthward,
Leant upon the hill.

Listening leant those silent Angels,
  And I also longed to hear
What sweet strain of earthly music
  Thus could charm their ear.

I heard the sound of many trumpets
  In a warlike march draw nigh;
Solemnly a mighty army
  Passed in order by.

But the clang had ceased; the echoes
  Soon had faded from the hill;
While the Angels, calm and earnest,
  Leant and listened still.

Then I heard a fainter clamour,
  Forge and wheel were clashing near.
And the Reapers in the meadow
  Singing loud and clear.

Listening Angels.

When the sunset came in glory,
    And the toil of day was o'er,
Still the Angels leant in silence,
    Listening as before.

Then, as daylight slowly vanished,
    And the evening mists grew dim
Solemnly from distant voices
    Rose a vesper hymn.

When the chant was done, and lingering
    Died upon the evening air,
From the hill the radiant Angels
    Still were listening there.

Silent came the gathering darkness,
    Bringing with it sleep and rest :
Save a little bird was singing
    Near her leafy nest.

Through the sounds of war and labour
    She had warbled all day long,
While the Angels leant and listened
    Only to her song.

But the starry night was coming ;
    When she ceased her little lay
From the mountain top the Angels
    Slowly passed away.

T

GOLDEN DAYS.

GOLDEN days—where are they?
　　Pilgrims east and west
　　Cry ; if we could find them
We would pause and rest :
We would pause and rest a little
　　From our long and weary ways :—
Where are they, then, where are they—
　　　　Golden days?

Golden days—where are they?
　　Ask of childhood's years,
Still untouched by sorrow,
　　Still undimmed by tears :
Ah, they seek a phantom Future,
　　Crowned with brighter, starry rays ;—
Where are they, then, where are they—
　　　　Golden days?

Golden days—where are they?
　　Has Love learnt the spell
That will charm them hither,
　　Near our hearth to dwell?
Insecure are all her treasures,
　　Restless is her anxious gaze :—
Where are they, then, where are they—
　　　　Golden days?

Golden days—where are they?
  Farther up the hill
I can hear the echo
  Faintly calling still :
Faintly calling, faintly dying,
  In a far-off misty haze :—
Where are they, then, where are they—
      Golden days?

PHILIP AND MILDRED.

LINGERING fade the rays of daylight, and
      the listening air is chilly ;
  Voice of bird and forest murmur, insect
      hum and quivering spray,
Stir not in that quiet hour : through the valley, calm
    and stilly,
  All in hushed and loving silence watch the slow
    departing Day.

Till the last faint western cloudlet, faint and rosy,
    ceases blushing,
  And the blue grows deep and deeper where one
    trembling planet shines,
And the day has gone for ever—then, like some great
    ocean rushing,
  The sad night wind wails lamenting, sobbing through
    the moaning pines.

Such, of all day's changing hours, is the fittest and the
meetest
For a farewell hour—and parting looks less bitter
and more blest ;
Earth seems like a shrine for sorrow, Nature's mother
voice is sweetest,
And her hand seems laid in chiding on the unquiet
throbbing breast.

Words are lower, for the twilight seems rebuking sad
repining,
And wild murmur and rebellion, as all childish and
in vain ;
Breaking through dark future hours clustering starry
hopes seem shining,
Then the calm and tender midnight folds her shadow
round the pain.

So they paced the shady lime-walk in that twilight dim
and holy,
Still the last farewell deferring, she could hear or he
should say ;
Every word, weighed down by sorrow, fell more tenderly and slowly—
This, which now beheld their parting, should have
been their wedding-day.

Should have been : her dreams of childhood, never
straying, never faltering,
Still had needed Philip's image to make future life
complete ;

Philip's young hopes of ambition, ever changing, ever
    altering,
  Needed Mildred's gentle presence even to make
    successes sweet.

This day should have seen their marriage ; the calm
    crowning and assurance
  Of two hearts, fulfilling rather, and not changing,
    either life :
Now they must be rent asunder, and her heart must
    learn endurance,
  For he leaves their home, and enters on a world of
    work and strife.

But her gentle spirit long had learnt, unquestioning,
    submitting,
  To revere his youthful longings, and to marvel at the
    fate
That gave such a humble office, all unworthy and un-
    fitting,
  To the genius of the village, who was born for some-
    thing great.

When the learnèd Traveller came there who had gained
    renown at college,
  Whose abstruse research had won him even Euro-
    pean fame,
Questioned Philip, praised his genius, marvelled at his
    self-taught knowledge,
  Could she murmur if he called him up to London
    and to fame ?

Could she waver when he bade her take the burden of
    decision,
  Since his troth to her was plighted, and his life was
    now her own?
Could she doom him to inaction? could she, when a
    newborn vision
  Rose in glory for his future, check it for her sake
    alone?

So her little trembling fingers, that had toiled with such
    fond pleasure,
  Paused, and laid aside, and folded the unfinished
    wedding gown;
Faltering earnestly assurance, that she too could, in her
    measure,
  Prize for him the present honour, and the future's
    sure renown.

Now they pace the shady lime-walk, now the last words
    must be spoken,
  Words of trust, for neither dreaded more than
    waiting and delay;
Was not love still called eternal—could a plighted vow
    be broken?—
  See the crimson light of sunset fades in purple mist
    away.

"Yes, my Mildred," Philip told her, "one calm thought
    of joy and blessing,
  Like a guardian spirit by me, through the world's
    tumultuous stir,

Still will spread its wings above me, and now urging,
    now repressing,
  With my Mildred's voice will murmur thoughts of
    home, and love, and her.

"It will charm my peaceful leisure, sanctify my daily
    toiling,
  With a right none else possesses, touching my heart's
    inmost string;
And to keep its pure wings spotless I shall fly the
    world's touch, soiling
  Even in thought this Angel Guardian of my Mildred's
    Wedding Ring.

"Take it, dear; this little circlet is the first link,
    strong and holy,
  Of a life-long chain, and holds me from all other
    love apart;
Till the day when you may wear it as my wife—my
    own—mine wholly—
  Let me know it rests for ever near the beating of
    your heart."

Dawn of day saw Philip speeding on his road to the
    Great City,
  Thinking how the stars gazed downward just with
    Mildred's patient eyes;
Dreams of work, and fame, and honour, struggling with
    a tender pity,
  Till the loving Past receding saw the conquering
    Future rise.

Daybreak still found Mildred watching, with the
    wonder of first sorrow,
  How the outward world unaltered shone the same
    this very day ;
How unpitying and relentless busy life met this new
    morrow,
  Earth, and sky, and man unheeding that her joy had
    passed away.

Then the round of weary duties, cold and formal, came
    to meet her,
  With the life within departed that had given them
    each a soul ;
And her sick heart even slighted gentle words that
    came to greet her ;
  For Grief spread its shadowy pinions, like a blight,
    upon the whole.

Jar one chord, the harp is silent ; move one stone, the
    arch is shattered ;
  One small clarion-cry of sorrow bids an armèd host
    awake ;
One dark cloud can hide the sunlight; loose one string,
    the pearls are scattered ;
  Think one thought, a soul may perish; say one
    word, a heart may break !

Life went on, the two lives running side by side; the
    outward seeming,
  And the truer and diviner hidden in the heart and
    brain ;

Dreams grow holy, put in action ; work grows fair
through starry dreaming;
But where each flows on unmingling, both are fruit-
less and in vain.

Such was Mildred's life ; her dreaming lay in some
far-distant region,
All the fairer, all the brighter, that its glories were
but guessed ;
And the daily round of duties seemed an unreal, airy
legion—
Nothing true save Philip's letters and the ring upon
her breast.

Letters telling how he struggled, for some plan or vision
aiming,
And at last how he just grasped it as a fresh one
spread its wings;
How the honour or the learning, once the climax,
now were claiming,
Only more and more, becoming merely steps to
higher things.

Telling her of foreign countries : little store had she of
learning,
So her earnest, simple spirit answered as he touched
the string;
Day by day, to these bright fancies all her silent
thoughts were turning,
Seeing every radiant picture framed within her
golden Ring.

Oh, poor heart—love, if thou willest; but, thine own
    soul still possessing,
  Live thy life: not a reflection or a shadow of his
    own:
Lean as fondly, as completely, as thou willest—but
    confessing
  That thy strength is God's, and therefore can, if
    need be, stand alone.

Little means were there around her to make farther,
    wider ranges,
  Where her loving gentle spirit could try any stronger
    flight;
And she turned aside, half fearing that fresh thoughts
    were fickle changes—
  That she *must* stay as he left her on that farewell
    summer night.

Love should still be guide and leader, like a herald
    should have risen,
  Lighting up the long dark vistas, conquering all
    opposing fates;
But new claims, new thoughts, new duties found her
    heart a silent prison,
  And found Love, with folded pinions, like a jailer
    by the gates.

Yet why blame her? it had needed greater strength
    than she was given
  To have gone against the current that so calmly
    flowed along;

Nothing fresh came near the village save the rain and
    dew of heaven,
  And her nature was too passive, and her love perhaps
    too strong.

The great world of thought, that rushes down the years,
    and onward sweeping
  Bears upon its mighty billows in its progress each
    and all,
Flowed so far away, its murmur did not rouse them
    from their sleeping;
  Life and Time and Truth were speaking, but they
    did not hear their call.

Years flowed on; and every morning heard her prayer
    grow lower, deeper,
  As she called all blessings on him, and bade every
    ill depart,
And each night when the cold moonlight shone upon
    that quiet sleeper,
  It would show her ring that glittered with each
    throbbing of her heart.

Years passed on. Fame came for Philip in a full,
    o'erflowing measure;
  He was spoken of and honoured through the breadth
    of many lands,
And he wrote it all to Mildred, as if praise were only
    pleasure,
  As if fame were only honour, when he laid them in
    her hands.

Mildred heard it without wonder, as a sure result ex-
  pected,
 For how could it fail, since merit and renown go side
  by side :
And the neighbours who first fancied genius ought to
  be suspected,
 Might at last give up their caution, and could own
  him now with pride.

Years flowed on. These empty honours led to others
  they called better,
 He had saved some slender fortune, and might claim
  his bride at last :
Mildred, grown so used to waiting, felt half startled by
  the letter
 That now made her future certain, and would con-
  secrate her past.

And he came : grown sterner, older—changed indeed :
  a grave reliance
 Had replaced his eager manner, and the quick short
  speech of old :
He had gone forth with a spirit half of hope and half
  defiance ;
 He returned with proud assurance half disdainful
  and half cold.

Yet his old self seemed returning while he stood sometimes, and listened
 To her calm soft voice, relating all the thoughts of
  these long years ;

And if Mildred's heart was heavy, and at times her blue
 eyes glistened,
  Still in thought she would not whisper aught of
  sorrow or of fears.

Autumn with its golden corn-fields, autumn with its
 storms and showers,
  Had been there to greet his coming with its forests
  gold and brown;
And the last leaves still were falling, fading still the
 year's last flowers,
  When he left the quiet village, and took back his
  bride to town.

Home—the home that she had pictured many a time
 in twilight, dwelling
  On that tender gentle fancy, folded round with loving
  care;
Here was home—the end, the haven; and what spirit
 voice seemed telling,
  That she only held the casket, with the gem no longer
  there?

Sad it may be to be longing, with a patience faint and
 weary,
  For a hope deferred—and sadder still to see it fade
  and fall;
Yet to grasp the thing we long for, and, with sorrow
 sick and dreary,
  Then to find how it can fail us, is the saddest pain
  of all.

What was wanting? He was gentle, kind, and generous
still, deferring
  To her wishes always ; nothing seemed to mar their
  tranquil life :
There are skies so calm and leaden that we long for
storm-winds stirring,
  There is peace so cold and bitter, that we almost
  welcome strife.

Darker grew the clouds above her, and the slow conviction clearer,
  That he gave her home and pity, but that heart, and
  soul, and mind
Were beyond her now ; he loved her, and in youth he
had been near her,
  But he now had gone far onward, and had left her
  there behind.

Yes, beyond her : yes, quick-hearted, her Love helped
her in revealing
  It was worthless, while so mighty ; was too weak,
  although so strong ;
There were courts she could not enter ; depths she
could not sound ; yet feeling
  It was vain to strive or struggle, vainer still to mourn
  or long.

He would give her words of kindness, he would talk of
home, but seeming
  With an absent look, forgetting if he held or dropped
  her hand ;

And then turn with eager pleasure to his writing, reading,
dreaming,
Or to speak of things with others that she could not
understand.

He had paid, and paid most nobly, all he owed; no
need of blaming;
It had cost him something, may be, that no future
could restore:
In her heart of hearts she knew it; Love and Sorrow,
not complaining,
Only suffered all the deeper, only loved him all the
more.

Sometimes then a stronger anguish, and more cruel,
weighed upon her,
That through all those years of waiting, he had slowly
learnt the truth;
He had known himself mistaken, but that, bound to
her in honour,
He renounced his life, to pay her for the patience of
her youth.

But a star was slowly rising from that mist of grief, and
brighter
Grew her eyes, for each slow hour surer comfort
seemed to bring;
And she watched with strange sad smiling, how her
trembling hands grew slighter,
And how thin her slender finger, and how large her
wedding-ring.

And the tears dropped slowly on it, as she kissed that
    golden token
  With a deeper love, it may be, than was in the far-
    off past ;
And remembering Philip's fancy, that so long ago was
    spoken,
  Thought her Ring's bright angel guardian had stayed
    near her to the last.

Grieving sorely, grieving truly, with a tender care and
    sorrow,
  Philip watched the slow, sure fading of his gentle,
    patient wife ;
Could he guess with what a yearning she was longing
    for the morrow,
  Could he guess the bitter knowledge that had wearied
    her of life ?

Now with violets strewn upon her, Mildred lies in
    peaceful sleeping ;
  All unbound her long, bright tresses, and her
    throbbing heart at rest,
And the cold, blue rays of moonlight, through the open
    casement creeping,
  Show the Ring upon her finger, and her hands crossed
    on her breast.

Peace at last. Of peace eternal is her calm sweet smile
    a token.
  Has some angel lingering near her let a radiant pro-
    mise fall ?

Has he told her Heaven unites again the links that
 Earth has broken?
For on Earth so much is needed, but in Heaven
 Love is all!

BORROWED THOUGHTS.

I. FROM "LAVATER."

TRUST him little who doth raise
 To one height both great and small,
And sets the sacred crown of praise,
 Smiling, on the head of all.

Trust him less who looks around
 To censure all with scornful eyes,
And in everything has found
 Something that he dare despise.

But for one who stands apart,
 Stirred by nought that can befall,
With a cold indifferent heart,—
 Trust him least and last of all.

II. FROM "PHANTASTES."

I HAVE a bitter Thought, a Snake
    That used to sting my life to pain.
I strove to cast it far away,
But every night and every day
    It crawled back to my heart again.

It was in vain to live or strive,
    To think or sleep, to work or pray;
At last I bade this thing accursed
Gnaw at my heart, and do its worst,
    And so I let it have its way.

Thus said I, "I shall never fall
    Into a false and dreaming peace,
And then awake, with sudden start,
To feel it biting at my heart,
    For now the pain can never cease."

But I gained more; for I have found
    That such a snake's envenomed charm
Must always, always find a part,
Deep in the centre of my heart,
    Which it can never wound or harm.

It is coiled round my heart to-day,
  It sleeps at times, this cruel snake,
And while it sleeps it never stings:—
Hush! let us talk of other things,
  Lest it should hear me and awake.

III. FROM "LOST ALICE."

YES, dear, our Love is slain;
  In the cold grave for evermore it lies,
    Never to wake again,
Or light our sorrow with its starry eyes:
    And so—regret is vain.

One hour of pain and dread,
We killed our Love, we took its life away
  With the false words we said;
And so we watch it, since that cruel day,
    Silent, and cold, and dead.

We should have seen it shine
Long years beside us. Time and Death might try
  To touch that life divine,
Whose strength could every other stroke defy
    Save only thine and mine.

No longing can restore
Our dead again.   Vain are the tears we weep,
And vainly we deplore
Our buried Love : its grave lies dark and deep
Between us evermore.

IV. FROM   *   *   *

WITHIN the kingdom of my Soul
I bid you enter, Love, to-day :
Submit my life to your control,
And give my Heart up to your sway.

My Past, whose light and life is flown,
Shall live through memory for you still ;
Take all my Present for your own,
And mould my Future to your will.

One only thought remains apart,
And will for ever so remain :
There is one Chamber in my heart
Where even you might knock in vain.

A haunted Chamber :—long ago
I closed it, and I cast the key
Where deep and bitter waters flow,
Into a vast and silent sea.

Dear, it is haunted.   All the rest
Is yours ; but I have shut that door
For ever now.   'Tis even best
That I should enter it no more.

No more.   It is not well to stay
With ghosts ; their very look would scare
Your joyous, loving smile away—
So never try to enter there.

Check, if you love me, all regret
That this one thought remains apart :—
Now let us smile, dear, and forget
The haunted Chamber in my Heart

LIGHT AND SHADE.

HOU hast done well to kneel and say,
    " Since He who gave can take away,
    And bid me suffer, I obey."

And also well to tell thy heart
That good lies in the bitterest part,
And thou wilt profit by her smart.

But bitter hours come to all :
When even truths like these will pall,
Sick hearts for humbler comfort call.

Then I would have thee strive to see
That good and evil come to thee,
As one of a great family.

And as material life is planned,
That even the loneliest one must stand
Dependent on his brother's hand;

So links more subtle and more fine
Bind every other soul to thine
In one great brotherhood divine.

Nor with thy share of work be vexed;
Though incomplete, and even perplext,
It fits exactly to the next.

What seems so dark to thy dim sight
May be a shadow, seen aright,
Making some brightness doubly bright.

The flash that struck thy tree,—no more
To shelter thee,—lets Heaven's blue floor
Shine where it never shone before.

Thy life that has been dropped aside
Into Time's stream, may stir the tide,
In rippled circles spreading wide.

The cry wrung from thy spirit's pain
May echo on some far-off plain,
And guide a wanderer home again.

Light and Shade.

Fail—yet rejoice; because no less
The failure that makes thy distress
May teach another full success.

It may be that in some great need
Thy life's poor fragments are decreed
To help build up a lofty deed.

Thy heart should throb in vast content,
Thus knowing that it was but meant
As chord in one great instrument;

That even the discord in thy soul
May make completer music roll
From out the great harmonious whole.

It may be, that when all is light,
Deep set within that deep delight
Will be to know *why* all was right;

To hear life's perfect music rise,
And while it floods the happy skies,
Thy feeble voice to recognise.

Then strive more gladly to fulfil
Thy little part.   This darkness still
Is light to every loving will.

And trust,—as if already plain,
How just thy share of loss and pain
Is for another fuller gain.

I dare not limit time or place
Touched by thy life : nor dare I trace
Its far vibrations into space.

One only knows.   Yet if the fret
Of thy weak heart, in weak regret
Needs a more tender comfort yet :

Then thou mayst take thy loneliest fears,
The bitterest drops of all thy tears,
The dreariest hours of all thy years ;

And through thy anguish there outspread,
May ask that God's great love would shed
Blessings on one belovèd head.

And thus thy soul shall learn to draw
Sweetness from out that loving law
That sees no failure and no flaw,

Where all is good.   And life is good,
Were the one lesson understood
Of its most sacred brotherhood.

A CHANGELING.

A LITTLE changeling spirit
 Crept to my arms one day :
I had no heart or courage
To drive the child away.

So all day long I soothed her,
 And hushed her on my breast ;
And all night long her wailing
 Would never let me rest.

I dug a grave to hold her,
 A grave both dark and deep ;
I covered her with violets,
 And laid her there to sleep.

I used to go and watch there,
 Both night and morning too :—
It was my tears, I fancy,
 That kept the violets blue.

I took her up : and once more
 I felt the clinging hold,
And heard the ceaseless wailing
 That wearied me of old.

I wandered, and I wandered,
  With my burden on my breast,
Till I saw a church-door open,
  And entered in to rest.

In the dim, dying daylight,
  Set in a flowery shrine,
I saw the Virgin Mother
  Holding her Child divine.

I knelt down there in silence,
  And on the Altar-stone
I laid my wailing burden,
  And came away—alone.

And now that little spirit,
  That sobbed so all day long,
Is grown a shining Angel,
  With wings both wide and strong

She watches me from Heaven,
  With loving, tender care,
And one day she has promised
  That I shall find her there.

DISCOURAGED.

WHERE the little babbling streamlet
　　First springs forth to light.
　Trickling through soft velvet mosses,
　Almost hid from sight ;
　Vowed I with delight,—
" River, I will follow thee,
Through thy wanderings to the Sea !"

Gleaming 'mid the purple heather.
　　Downward then it sped,
Glancing through the mountain gorges,
　　Like a silver thread,
　　As it quicker fled,
Louder music in its flow,
Dashing to the Vale below.

Then its voice grew lower, gentler,
　　And its pace less fleet,
Just as though it loved to linger
　　Round the rushes' feet,
　　As they stooped to meet
Their clear images below,
Broken by the ripples' flow.

Purple Willow-herb bent over
  To her shadow fair;
Meadow-sweet, in feathery clusters,
  Perfumed all the air;
  Silver-weed was there,
And in one calm, grassy spot,
Starry, blue Forget-me-not.

Tangled weeds, below the waters,
  Still seemed drawn away;
Yet the current, floating onward,
  Was less strong than they;—
  Sunbeams watched their play,
With a flickering light and shade,
Through the screen the Alders made.

Broader grew the flowing River;
  To its grassy brink;
Slowly, in the slanting sun-rays,
  Cattle trooped to drink:
  The blue sky, I think,
Was no bluer than that stream,
Slipping onward, like a dream.

Quicker, deeper then it hurried,
  Rushing fierce and free;
But I said, " It should grow calmer
  Ere it meets the Sea,
  The wide purple Sea,
Which I weary for in vain,
Wasting all my toil and pain."

But it rushed still quicker, fiercer,
   In its rocky bed,
Hard and stony was the pathway
   To my tired tread ;
   " I despair," I said,
" Of that wide and glorious Sea,
That was promised unto me."

So I turned aside, and wandered
   Through green meadows near,
Far away, among the daisies,
   Far away, for fear
   Lest I still should hear
The loud murmur of its song,
As the River flowed along.

Now I hear it not :—I loiter
   Gaily as before ;
Yet I sometimes think,—and thinking
   Makes my heart so sore,—
   Just a few steps more,
And there might have shone for me,
Blue and infinite, the Sea.

IF THOU COULDST KNOW.

 THINK if thou couldst know,
  Oh soul that will complain,
 What lies concealed below
  Our burden and our pain;
 How just our anguish brings
 Nearer those longed-for things
 We seek for now in vain,—
I think thou wouldst rejoice, and not complain.

 I think if thou couldst see,
  With thy dim mortal sight,
 How meanings, dark to thee,
  Are shadows hiding light;
 Truth's efforts crossed and vexed,
 Life's purpose all perplexed,—
 If thou couldst see them right,
I think that they would seem all clear, and wise, and
 bright.

 And yet thou canst not know,
  And yet thou canst not see;
 Wisdom and sight are slow
  In poor humanity.

If thou couldst *trust*, poor soul,
In Him who rules the whole,
Thou wouldst find peace and rest :
Wisdom and sight are well, but Trust is best.

THE WARRIOR TO HIS DEAD BRIDE.

IF in the fight my arm was strong,
  And forced my foes to yield,
If conquering and unhurt I came
Back from the battle-field—
It is because thy prayers have been
My safeguard and my shield.

My comrades smile to see my arm
  Spare or protect a foe,
They think thy gentle pleading voice
  Was silenced long ago ;
But pity and compassion, love,
  Were taught me first by woe.

Thy heart, my own, still beats in Heaven
  With the same love divine
That made thee stoop to such a soul,
  So hard, so stern, as mine—
My eyes have learnt to weep, beloved,
  Since last they looked on thine.

I hear thee murmur words of peace
   Through the dim midnight air,
And a calm falls from the angel stars
   And soothes my great despair—
The Heavens themselves look brighter, love,
   Since thy sweet soul is there.

And if my heart is once more calm,
   My step is once more free,
It is because each hour I feel
   Thou prayest still for me;
Because no fate or change can come
   Between my soul and thee.

It is because my heart is stilled,
   Not broken by despair,
Because I see the grave is bright,
   And death itself is fair—
I dread no more the wrath of Heaven—
   I have an angel there!

A LETTER

EAR, I tried to write you such a letter
As would tell you all my heart to-day.
Written Love is poor; one word were
    better;
Easier, too, a thousand times, to say.

I can tell you all: fears, doubts unheeding,
While I can be near you, hold your hand,
Looking right into your eyes, and reading
Reassurance that you understand.

Yet I wrote it through, then lingered, thinking
Of its reaching you,—what hour, what day;
Till I felt my heart and courage sinking
With a strange, new, wondering dismay.

" Will my letter fall," I wondered sadly,
" On her mood like some discordant tone,
Or be welcomed tenderly and gladly?
Will she be with others, or alone?

" It may find her too absorbed to read it,
Save with hurried glance and careless air:
Sad and weary, she may scarcely heed it;
Gay and happy, she may hardly care.

" Shall I—dare I—risk the chances?" slowly
Something,—was it shyness, love, or pride?—
Chilled my heart, and checked my courage wholly;
So I laid it wistfully aside.

Then I leant against the casement, turning
Tearful eyes towards the far-off west,
Where the golden evening light was burning,
Till my heart throbbed back again to rest.

And I thought : " Love's soul is not in fetters,
Neither space nor time keep souls apart ;
Since I cannot—dare not—send my letters,
Through the silence I will send my heart.

" If, perhaps now, while my tears are falling,
She is dreaming quietly alone,
She will hear my Love's far echo calling,
Feel my spirit drawing near her own.

" She will hear, while twilight shades enfold her,
All the gathered Love she knows so well—
Deepest Love my words have ever told her,
Deeper still—all I could never tell.

" Wondering at the strange mysterious power
That has touched her heart, then she will say :—
' Some one whom I love, this very hour,
Thinks of me, and loves me, far away.'

" If, as well may be, to-night has found her
Full of other thoughts, with others by,
Through the words and claims that gather round her
She will hear just one, half-smothered sigh ;

" Or will marvel why, without her seeking
Suddenly the thought of me recurs ;
Or, while listening to another speaking,
Fancy that my hand is holding hers."

So I dreamed, and watched the stars' far splendour
Glimmering on the azure darkness, start,—
While the star of trust rose bright and tender,
Through the twilight shadows of my heart.

A COMFORTER.

I.

WILL she come to me, little Effie,
    Will she come in my arms to rest,
    And nestle her head on my shoulder,
While the sun goes down in the west ?

II.

" I and Effie will sit together,
    All alone, in this great arm-chair :—
Is it silly to mind it, darling,
    When Life is so hard to bear ?

III.

" No one comforts me like my Effie,
Just I think that she does not try,—
Only looks with a wistful wonder
Why grown people should ever cry ;

IV.

"While her little soft arms close tighter
Round my neck in their clinging hold :—
Well, I must not cry on your hair, dear,
For my tears might tarnish the gold.

V.

" I am tired of trying to read, dear ;
It is worse to talk and seem gay :
There are some kinds of sorrow, Effie,
It is useless to thrust away.

VI.

" Ah, advice may be wise, my darling,
But one always knows it before ;
And the reasoning down one's sorrow
Seems to make one suffer the more.

VII.

" But my Effie won't reason, will she ?
Or endeavour to understand ;
Only holds up her mouth to kiss me,
As she strokes my face with her hand.

VIII.

" If you break your plaything yourself, dear,
    Don't you cry for it all the same?
I don't think it is such a comfort,
    One has only oneself to blame.

IX.

" People say things cannot be helped, dear,
    But then that is the reason why ;
For if things could be helped or altered,
    One would never sit down to cry :

X.

" They say, too, that tears are quite useless
    To undo, amend, or restore,—
When I think *how* useless, my Effie,
    Then my tears only fall the more.

XI.

" All to-day I struggled against it ;
    But that does not make sorrow cease ;
And now, dear, it is such a comfort
    To be able to cry in peace.

XII.

" Though wise people would call that folly,
    And remonstrate with grave surprise;
We won't mind what they say, my Effie ;—
    We never professed to be wise.

XIII.

" But my comforter knows a lesson
   Wiser, truer than all the rest :—
That to help and to heal a sorrow,
   Love and silence are always best.

XIV.

" Well, who is my comforter—tell me ?
   Effie smiles, but she will not speak ;
Or look up through the long curled lashes
   That are shading her rosy cheek.

XV.

" Is she thinking of talking fishes,
   The blue bird, or magical tree ?
Perhaps I am thinking, my darling,
   Of something that never can be.

XVI.

" You long—don't you, dear ?—for the Genii,
   Who were slaves of lamps and of rings ;
And I—I am sometimes afraid, dear,—
   I want as impossible things.

XVII.

" But hark ! there is Nurse calling Effie !
   It is bedtime, so run away,
And I must go back, or the others
   Will be wondering why I stay.

XVIII.

" So good-night to my darling Effie ;
   Keep happy, sweetheart, and grow wise : --
There's one kiss for her golden tresses,
   And two for her sleepy eyes."

UNSEEN.

THERE are more things in Heaven and Earth,
     than we
  Can dream of, or than nature understands ;
We learn not through our poor philosophy
What hidden chords are touched by unseen hands.

The present hour repeats upon its strings
Echoes of some vague dream we have forgot ;
Dim voices whisper half-remembered things,
And when we pause to listen,—answer not.

Forebodings come : we know not how, or whence,
Shadowing a nameless fear upon the soul,
And stir within our hearts a subtler sense,
Than light may read, or wisdom may control.

And who can tell what secret links of thought
Bind heart to heart ? Unspoken things are heard,
As if within our deepest selves was brought
The soul, perhaps, of some unuttered word.

But, though a veil of shadow hangs between
That hidden life, and what we see and hear,
Let us revere the power of the Unseen,
And know a world of mystery is near.

A REMEMBRANCE OF AUTUMN.

OTHING stirs the sunny silence,—
    Save the drowsy humming of the bees
      Round the rich, ripe peaches on
        the wall,
And the south wind sighing in the trees,
    And the dead leaves rustling as they fall :
While the swallows, one by one, are gathering,
    All impatient to be on the wing,
And to wander from us, seeking
         Their belovèd Spring !

Cloudless rise the azure heavens !
    Only vaporous wreaths of snowy white
      Nestle in the grey hill's rugged side ;
    And the golden woods are bathed in light,
      Dying, if they must, with kingly pride :
While the swallows in the blue air wheeling,
    Circle now an eager fluttering band,
Ready to depart and leave us
         For a brighter land !

But a voice is sounding sadly,
  Telling of a glory that has been ;
  Of a day that faded all too fast—
See afar through the blue air serene,
  Where the swallows wing their way at last,
And our hearts perchance, as sadly wandering,
  Vainly seeking for a long-lost day,
While we watch the far-off swallows,
          Flee with them away !

THREE EVENINGS IN A LIFE.

I.

YES, it looked dark and dreary,
    That long and narrow street :
  Only the sound of the rain,
  And the tramp of passing feet,
The duller glow of the fire,
  And gathering mists of night
To mark how slow and weary
  The long day's cheerless flight !

II.

Watching the sullen fire,
  Hearing the dismal rain,
Drop after drop, run down
  On the darkening window-pane :

Chill was the heart of Alice,
   Chill as that winter day,—
For the star of her life had risen
   Only to fade away.

III.

The voice that had been so strong
   To bid the snare depart,
The true and earnest will,
   The calm and steadfast heart,
Were now weighed down by sorrow,
   Were quivering now with pain;
The clear path now seemed clouded,
   And all her grief in vain.

IV.

Duty, Right, Truth, who promised
   To help and save their own,
Seemed spreading wide their pinions
   To leave her there alone.
So, turning from the Present
   To well-known days of yore,
She called on them to strengthen
   And guard her soul once more.

V.

She thought how in her girlhood
   Her life was given away,
The solemn promise spoken
   She kept so well to-day;

How to her brother Herbert
　　She had been help and guide,
And how his artist nature
　　On her calm strength relied.

VI.

How through life's fret and turmoil
　　The passion and fire of art
In him was soothed and quickened
　　By her true sister heart;
How future hopes had always
　　Been for his sake alone;
And now,—what strange new feeling
　　Possessed her as its own?

VII.

Her home—each flower that breathed there,
　　The wind's sigh, soft and low,
Each trembling spray of ivy,
　　The river's murmuring flow,
The shadow of the forest,
　　Sunset, or twilight dim—
Dear as they were, were dearer
　　By leaving them for him.

VIII.

And each year as it found her
　　In the dull, feverish town,
Saw self still more forgotten,
　　And selfish care kept down

By the calm joy of evening
　　That brought him to her side,
To warn him with wise counsel,
　　Or praise with tender pride.

IX.

Her heart, her life, her future,
　　Her genius, only meant
Another thing to give him,
　　And be therewith content.
To-day, what words had stirred her,
　　Her soul could not forget?
What dream had filled her spirit
　　With strange and wild regret?

X.

To leave him for another,—
　　Could it indeed be so?
Could it have cost such anguish
　　To bid this vision go?
Was this her faith?　Was Herbert
　　The second in her heart?
Did it need all this struggle
　　To bid a dream depart?

XI.

And yet, within her spirit
　　A far-off land was seen,
A home, which might have held her,
　　A love, which might have been.

And Life—not the mere being
  Of daily ebb and flow,
But Life itself had claimed her,
  And she had let it go !

XII.

Within her heart there echoed
  Again the well-known tone
That promised this bright future,
  And asked her for her own :
Then words of sorrow, broken
  By half-reproachful pain ;
And then a farewell, spoken
  In words of cold disdain.

XIII.

Where now was the stern purpose
  That nerved her soul so long ?
Whence came the words she uttered,
  So hard, so cold, so strong ?
What right had she to banish
  A hope that God had given ?
Why must she choose earth's portion,
  And turn aside from Heaven ?

XIV.

To-day ! Was it this morning ?
  If this long, fearful strife
Was but the work of hours,
  What would be years of life ?

Why did a cruel Heaven
　　For such great suffering call?
And why—Oh, still more cruel!—
　　Must her own words do all?

XV.

Did she repent? Oh Sorrow
　　Why do we linger still
To take thy loving message,
　　And do thy gentle will?
See, her tears fall more slowly,
　　The passionate murmurs cease,
And back upon her spirit
　　Flow strength, and love, and peace.

XVI.

The fire burns more brightly,
　　The rain has passed away,
Herbert will see no shadow
　　Upon his home to-day;
Only that Alice greets him
　　With doubly tender care,
Kissing a fonder blessing
　　Down on his golden hair.

II.

I.

THE Studio is deserted,
   Palette and brush laid by,
   The sketch rests on the easel,
   The paint is scarcely dry ;
And Silence—who seems always
   Within her depths to bear
The next sound that will utter—
   Now holds a dumb despair.

II.

So Alice feels it : listening
   With breathless, stony fear,
Waiting the dreadful summons
   Each minute brings more near :
When the young life, now ebbing,
   Shall fail, and pass away
Into that mighty shadow
   Who shrouds the house to-day.

III.

But why—when the sick chamber
   Is on the upper floor—
Why dares not Alice enter
   Within the close-shut door ?

If he—her all—her Brother,
　　Lies dying in that gloom,
What strange mysterious power
　　Has sent her from the room?

IV.

It is not one week's anguish
　　That can have changed her so;
Joy has not died here lately,
　　Struck down by one quick blow;
But cruel months have needed
　　Their long relentless chain,
To teach that shrinking manner
　　Of helpless, hopeless pain.

V.

The struggle was scarce over
　　Last Christmas Eve had brought:
The fibres still were quivering
　　Of the one wounded thought,
When Herbert—who, unconscious,
　　Had guessed no inward strife—
Bade her, in pride and pleasure,
　　Welcome his fair young wife.

VI.

Bade her rejoice, and smiling,
　　Although his eyes were dim,
Thanked God he thus could pay her
　　The care she gave to him.

This fresh bright life would bring her
  A new and joyous fate—
Oh, Alice, check the murmur
  That cries, " Too late ! too late !"

VII.

Too late ! Could she have known it
  A few short weeks before,
That his life was completed,
  And needing hers no more,
She might——Oh sad repining !
  What " might have been," forget ·
" It was not," should suffice us
  To stifle vain regret.

VIII.

He needed her no longer,
  Each day it grew more plain ;
First with a startled wonder,
  Then with a wondering pain.
Love : why, his wife best gave it ;
  Comfort : durst Alice speak,
Or counsel, when resentment
  Flushed on the young wife's cheek ?

IX.

No more long talks by firelight
  Of childish times long past,
And dreams of future greatness
  Which he must reach at last ;

Y

Dreams, where her purer instinct
  With truth unerring told,
Where was the worthless gilding,
  And where refinèd gold.

X.

Slowly, but surely ever,
  Dora's poor jealous pride,
Which she called love for Herbert,
  Drove Alice from his side;
And, spite of nervous effort
  To share their altered life,
She felt a check to Herbert,
  A burden to his wife.

XI.

This was the least; for Alice
  Feared, dreaded, *knew* at length
How much his nature owed her
  Of truth, and power, and strength;
And watched the daily failing
  Of all his nobler part:
Low aims, weak purpose, telling
  In lower, weaker art.

XII.

And now, when he is dying,
  The last words she could hear
Must not be hers, but given
  The bride of one short year.

The last care is another's;
   The last prayer must not be
The one they learnt together
   Beside their mother's knee.

XIII.

Summoned at last: she kisses
   The clay-cold stiffening hand;
And, reading pleading efforts
   To make her understand,
Answers, with solemn promise,
   In clear but trembling tone,
To Dora's life henceforward
   She will devote her own.

XIV.

Now all is over.   Alice
   Dares not remain to weep,
But soothes the frightened Dora
   Into a sobbing sleep.
The poor weak child will need her: . . .
   Oh, who can dare complain,
When God sends a new Duty
   To comfort each new Pain!

III.

I.

THE House is all deserted
  In the dim evening gloom
Only one figure passes
  Slowly from room to room;
And, pausing at each doorway,
  Seems gathering up again
Within her heart the relics
  Of bygone joy and pain.

II.

There is an earnest longing
  In those who onward gaze,
Looking with weary patience
  Towards the coming days.
There is a deeper longing,
  More sad, more strong, more keen:
Those know it who look backward,
  And yearn for what has been.

III.

At every hearth she pauses,
  Touches each well-known chair;
Gazes from every window,
  Lingers on every stair.

What have these months brought Alice
   Now one more year is past?
This Christmas Eve shall tell us,
   The third one and the last.

IV.

The wilful, wayward Dora,
   In those first weeks of grief,
Could seek and find in Alice
   Strength, soothing, and relief;
And Alice—last sad comfort
   True woman-heart can take—
Had something still to suffer
   And bear for Herbert's sake.

V.

Spring, with her western breezes,
   From Indian islands bore
To Alice news that Leonard
   Would seek his home once more.
What was it—joy, or sorrow?
   What were they—hopes, or fears?
That flushed her cheeks with crimson,
   And filled her eyes with tears?

VI.

He came.   And who so kindly
   Could ask and hear her tell
Herbert's last hours; for Leonard
   Had known and loved him well.

Daily he came; and Alice,
  Poor weary heart, at length,
Weighed down by others' weakness,
  Could lean upon his strength.

VII.

Yet not the voice of Leonard
  Could her true care beguile,
That turned to watch, rejoicing,
  Dora's reviving smile.
So, from that little household
  The worst gloom passed away,
The one bright hour of evening
  Lit up the livelong day.

VIII.

Days passed.   The golden summer
  In sudden heat bore down
Its blue, bright, glowing sweetness
  Upon the scorching town.
And sights and sounds of country
  Came in the warm soft tune
Sung by the honeyed breezes
  Borne on the wings of June.

IX.

One twilight hour, but earlier
  Than usual, Alice thought
She knew the fresh sweet fragrance
  Of flowers that Leonard brought;

Through opened doors and windows
　It stole up through the gloom,
And with appealing sweetness
　Drew Alice from her room.

x.

Yes, he was there ; and pausing
　Just near the opened door,
To check her heart's quick beating,
　She heard—and paused still more—
His low voice—Dora's answers—
　His pleading—Yes, she knew
The tone—the words—the accents :
　She once had heard them too.

xi.

" Would Alice blame her ? " Leonard's
　Low, tender answer came :—
" Alice was far too noble
　To think or dream of blame."
" And was he sure he loved her ? "
　" Yes, with the one love given
Once in a lifetime only,
　With one soul and one heaven ! "

xii.

Then came a plaintive murmur,—
　" Dora had once been told
That he and Alice "—— " Dearest,
　Alice is far too cold

To love; and I, my Dora,
  If once I fancied so,
It was a brief delusion,
  And over,—long ago."

XIII.

Between the Past and Present,
  On that bleak moment's height,
She stood.   As some lost traveller
  By a quick flash of light
Seeing a gulf before him,
  With dizzy, sick despair,
Reels backward, but to find it
  A deeper chasm there.

XIV.

The twilight grew still darker,
  The fragrant flowers more sweet,
The stars shone out in heaven,
  The lamps gleamed down the street;
And hours passed in dreaming
  Over their new-found fate,
Ere they could think of wondering
  Why Alice was so late.

XV.

She came, and calmly listened;
  In vain they strove to trace
If Herbert's memory shadowed
  In grief upon her face.

No blame, no wonder showed there,
　No feeling could be told;
Her voice was not less steady,
　Her manner not more cold.

XVI.

They could not hear the anguish
　That broke in words of pain
Through the calm summer midnight,—
　" My Herbert—mine again !"
Yes, they have once been parted,
　But this day shall restore
The long lost one : she claims him :
　" My Herbert—mine once more !"

XVII.

Now Christmas Eve returning,
　Saw Alice stand beside
The altar, greeting Dora,
　Again a smiling bride;
And now the gloomy evening
　Sees Alice pale and worn,
Leaving the house for ever,
　To wander out forlorn.

XVIII.

Forlorn—nay, not so.　Anguish
　Shall do its work at length;
Her soul, passed through the fire,
　Shall gain still purer strength.

Somewhere there waits for Alice
An earnest noble part ;
And, meanwhile God is with her,—
God, and her own true heart !

THE WIND.

THE wind went forth o'er land and sea
Loud and free ;
Foaming waves leapt up to meet it,
Stately pines bowed down to greet it ;
While the wailing sea
And the forest's murmured sigh
Joined the cry
Of the wind that swept o'er land and sea.

The wind that blew upon the sea
Fierce and free,
Cast the bark upon the shore,
Whence it sailed the night before
Full of hope and glee !
And the cry of pain and death
Was but a breath,
Through the wind that roared upon the sea.

The wind was whispering on the lea
Tenderly ;

But the white rose felt it pass,
And the fragile stalks of grass
    Shook with fear to see
All her trembling petals shed,
    As it fled,
So gently by,—the wind upon the lea.

Blow, thou wind, upon the sea
    Fierce and free,
And a gentler message send,
Where frail flowers and grasses bend,
    On the sunny lea ;
For thy bidding still is one,
    Be it done
In tenderness or wrath, on land or sea !

EXPECTATION.

THE King's three daughters stood on the
    terrace,
    The hanging terrace, so broad and green,
Which keeps the sea from the marble Palace,
There was Princess May, and Princess Alice,
And the youngest Princess, Gwendoline.

Sighed Princess May, " Will it last much longer.
Time throbs so slow and my Heart so quick ;

And oh, how long is the day in dying;
Weary am I of waiting and sighing,
For Hope deferred makes the spirit sick."

But Princess Gwendoline smiled and kissed her :—
"Am I not sadder than you, my Sister?
Expecting joy is a happy pain.
The Future's fathomless mine of treasures
All countless hordes of possible pleasures,
Might bring their store to my feet in vain."

Sighed Princess Alice as night grew nearer :—
"So soon, so soon, is the daylight fled!
And oh, how fast comes the dark to-morrow,
Who hides, perhaps in her veil of sorrow,
The terrible hour I wait and dread!"

But Princess Gwendoline kissed her, sighing,—
"It is only Life that can fear dying;
Possible loss means possible gain.
Those who still dread, are not quite forsaken;
But not to fear, because all is taken,
Is the loneliest depth of human pain."

AN IDEAL.

WHILE the grey mists of early dawn
   Were lingering round the hill,
   And the dew was still upon the flowers,
  And the earth lay calm and still,
A wingèd Spirit came to me,
Noble, and radiant, and free.

Folding his blue and shining wings,
   He laid his hand on mine.
I know not if I felt, or heard
   The mystic word divine,
Which woke the trembling air to sighs,
And shone from out his starry eyes.

The word he spoke, within my heart
   Stirred life unknown before,
And cast a spell upon my soul
   To chain it evermore;
Making the cold dull earth look bright,
And skies flame out in sapphire light.

When noon ruled from the heavens, and man
   Through busy day toiled on,
My Spirit drooped his shining wings;
   His radiant smile was gone;

His voice had ceased, his grace had flown,
His hand grew cold within my own.

Bitter, oh bitter tears, I wept,
   Yet still I held his hand,
Hoping with vague unreasoning hope :
   I would not understand
That this pale Spirit never more
Could be what he had been before.

Could it be so ?   My heart stood still.
   Yet he was by my side.
I strove ; but my despair was vain ;
   Vain, too, was love and pride.
Could he have changed to me so soon ?
My day was only at its noon.

Now stars are rising one by one,
   Through the dim evening air ;
Near me a household Spirit waits,
   With tender loving care ;
He speaks and smiles, but never sings,
Long since he lost his shining wings.

With thankful, true content, I know
   This is the better way ;
Is not a faithful spirit mine—
   Mine still—at close of day ? . . . .
Yet will my foolish heart repine
For that bright morning dream of mine.

OUR DEAD.

NOTHING is our own : we hold our pleasures
Just a little while, ere they are fled :
One by one life robs us of our treasures :
Nothing is our own except our Dead.

They are ours, and hold in faithful keeping
Safe for ever, all they took away.
Cruel life can never stir that sleeping,
Cruel time can never seize that prey.

Justice pales ; truth fades ; stars fall from Heaven ;
Human are the great whom we revere :
No true crown of honour can be given,
Till we place it on a funeral bier.

How the Children leave us : and no traces
Linger of that smiling angel band ;
Gone, for ever gone ; and in their places,
Weary men and anxious women stand.

Yet we have some little ones, still ours ;
They have kept the baby smile we know,
Which we kissed one day, and hid with flowers,
On their dead white faces, long ago.

When our Joy is lost—and life will take it—
Then no memory of the past remains;
Save with some strange, cruel sting, to make it
Bitterness beyond all present pains.

Death, more tender-hearted, leaves to sorrow
Still the radiant shadow, fond regret:
We shall find, in some far, bright to-morrow,
Joy that he has taken, living yet.

Is Love ours, and do we dream we know it,
Bound with all our heart-strings, all our own?
Any cold and cruel dawn may show it,
Shattered, desecrated, overthrown.

Only the dead Hearts forsake us never;
Death's last kiss has been the mystic sign
Consecrating Love our own for ever,
Crowning it eternal and divine.

So when Fate would fain besiege our city,
Dim our gold, or make our flowers fall,
Death, the Angel, comes in love and pity,
And to save our treasures, claims them all.

A WOMAN'S ANSWER.

I WILL not let you say a Woman's part
    Must be to give exclusive love alone ;
Dearest, although I love you so, my heart
Answers a thousand claims besides your own.

I love—what do I not love ? earth and air
    Find space within my heart, and myriad things
You would not deign to heed, are cherished there,
    And vibrate on its very inmost strings.

I love the summer with her ebb and flow
    Of light, and warmth, and music that have nurst
Her tender buds to blossoms . . . and you know
    It was in summer that I saw you first.

I love the winter dearly too, ... but then
    I owe it so much ; on a winter's day,
Bleak, cold, and stormy, you returned again,
    When you had been those weary months away.

I love the Stars like friends ; so many nights
    I gazed at them, when you were far from me,
Till I grew blind with tears . . . . those far off lights
    Could watch you, whom I longed in vain to see.

I love tnc Flowers ; happy hours lie
    Shut up within their petals close and fast :

z

You have forgotten, dear : but they and I
　　Keep every fragment of the golden Past.

I love, too, to be loved ; all loving praise
　　Seems like a crown upon my Life,—to make
It better worth the giving, and to raise
　　Still nearer to your own the heart you take.

I love all good and noble souls ;—I heard
　　One speak of you but lately, and for days
Only to think of it, my soul was stirred
　　In tender memory of such generous praise.

I love all those who love you ; all who owe
　　Comfort to you : and I can find regret
Even for those poorer hearts who once could know,
　　And once could love you, and can now forget.

Well, is my heart so narrow—I, who spare
　　Love for all these ?　Do I not even hold
My favourite books in special tender care,
　　And prize them as a miser does his gold?

The Poets that you used to read to me
　　While summer twilights faded in the sky ;
But most of all I think Aurora Leigh,
　　Because—because—do you remember why?

Will you be jealous ?　Did you guess before
　　I loved so many things?—Still you the best :—
Dearest, remember that I love you more,
　　Oh, more a thousand times than all the rest !

THE STORY OF THE FAITHFUL SOUL.

FOUNDED ON AN OLD FRENCH LEGEND.

THE fettered Spirits linger
   In purgatorial pain,
With penal fires effacing
   Their last faint earthly stain,
Which Life's imperfect sorrow
   Had tried to cleanse in vain.

Yet, on each feast of Mary
   Their sorrow finds release,
For the Great Archangel Michael
   Comes down and bids it cease;
And the name of these brief respites
   Is called "Our Lady's Peace."

Yet once—so runs the Legend—
   When the Archangel came
And all these holy spirits
   Rejoiced at Mary's name;
One voice alone was wailing,
   Still wailing on the same.

And though a great Te Deum
   The happy echoes woke,
This one discordant wailing
   Through the sweet voices broke:

So when St. Michael questioned
  Thus the poor spirit spoke :—

" I am not cold or thankless,
  Although I still complain ;
I prize our Lady's blessing,
  Although it comes in vain
To still my bitter anguish,
  Or quench my ceaseless pain.

" On earth a heart that loved me
  Still lives and mourns me there,
And the shadow of his anguish
  Is more than I can bear ;
All the torment that I suffer
  Is the thought of his despair.

" The evening of my bridal
  Death took my Life away ;
Not all Love's passionate pleading
  Could gain an hour's delay.
And he I left has suffered
  A whole year since that day.

" If I could only see him,—
  If I could only go
And speak one word of comfort
  And solace,—then, I know
He would endure with patience,
  And strive against his woe."

Thus the Archangel answered :—
  " Your time of pain is brief,
And soon the peace of Heaven
  Will give you full relief;
Yet if his earthly comfort
  So much outweighs your grief,

" Then through a special mercy
  I offer you this grace,—
You may seek him who mourns you
  And look upon his face,
And speak to him of comfort
  For one short minute's space.

" But when that time is ended,
  Return here, and remain
A thousand years in torment,
  A thousand years in pain :
Thus dearly must you purchase
  The comfort he will gain."

         *   *   *   *

The Lime-trees' shade at evening
  Is spreading broad and wide ;
Beneath their fragrant arches,
  Pace slowly, side by side,
In low and tender converse,
  A Bridegroom and his Bride.

The night is calm and stilly,
　No other sound is there
Except their happy voices:
　What is that cold bleak air
That passes through the Lime-trees
　And stirs the Bridegroom's hair?

While one low cry of anguish,
　Like the last dying wail
Of some dumb, hunted creature,
　Is borne upon the gale :—
Why does the Bridegroom shudder
　And turn so deathly pale?

*　　*　　*

Near Purgatory's entrance
　The radiant Angels wait ;
It was the great St. Michael
　Who closed that gloomy gate
When the poor wandering spirit
　Came back to meet her fate.

" Pass on," thus spoke the Angel :
　" Heaven's joy is deep and vast ;
Pass on, pass on, poor Spirit,
　For Heaven is yours at last ;
In that one minute's anguish
　Your thousand years have passed."

A CONTRAST.

CAN you open that ebony casket?
　　Look, this is the key: but stay,
Those are only a few old letters
Which I keep,—to burn some day.

Yes, that Locket is quaint and ancient;
　　But leave it, dear, with the ring,
And give me the little Portrait
　　Which hangs by a crimson string.

I have never opened that Casket
　　Since, many long years ago,
It was sent me back in anger
　　By one whom I used to know.

But I want you to see the Portrait:
　　I wonder if you can trace
A look of that smiling creature
　　Left now in my faded face.

It was like me once; but remember
　　The weary relentless years,
And Life, with its fierce, brief Tempests.
　　And its long, long rain of tears.

Is it strange to call it my Portrait?
  Nay, smile, dear, for well you may,
To think of that radiant Vision
  And of what I am to-day.

With restless, yet confident longing
  How those blue eyes seem to gaze
Into deep and exhaustless Treasures,
  All hid in the coming days.

With that trust which leans on the Future,
  And counts on her promised store,
Until she has taught us to tremble
  And hope,—but to trust no more.

How that young, light heart would have pitied
  Me now—if her dreams had shown
A quiet and weary woman
  With all her illusions flown.

Yet I—who shall soon be resting,
  And have passed the hardest part,
Can look back with a deeper pity
  On that young unconscious heart.

It is strange; but Life's currents drift us
  So surely and swiftly on,
That we scarcely notice the changes,
  And how many things are gone:

And forget, while to-day absorbs us,
   How old mysteries are unsealed;
How the old, old ties are loosened,
   And the old, old wounds are healed.

And we say that our Life is fleeting
   Like a story that Time has told;
But we fancy that we—we only
   Are just what we were of old.

So now and then it is wisdom
   To gaze, as I do to-day,
At a half-forgotten relic
   Of a Time that is passed away.

The very look of that Portrait,
   The Perfume that seems to cling
To those fragile and faded letters,
   And the Locket, and the Ring,

If they only stirred in my spirit
   Forgotten pleasure and pain,—
Why, memory is often bitter,
   And almost always in vain;

But the contrast of bygone hours
   Comes to rend a veil away,—
And I marvel to see the stranger
   Who is living in me to-day.

THE BRIDE'S DREAM.

THE stars are gleaming;
  The maiden sleeps—
What is she dreaming?
For see—she weeps.
By her side is an Angel
  With folded wings;
While the Maiden slumbers
  The Angel sings:
He sings of a Bridal,
  Of Love, of Pain,
Of a heart to be given,—
  And all in vain;
(See, her cheek is flushing,
  As if with pain;)
He telleth of sorrow,
  Regrets and fears,
And the few vain pleasures
  We buy with tears;
And the bitter lesson
  We learn from years.

The stars are gleaming
  Upon her brow:
What is she dreaming
  So calmly now?

By her side is the Angel
  With folded wings ;
She smiles in her slumber
  The while he sings.
He sings of a Bridal,
  Of Love divine ;
Of a heart to be laid
  On a sacred shrine ;
Of a crown of glory,
  Where seraphs shine ;
Of the deep, long rapture
  The chosen know
Who forsake for Heaven
  Vain joys below,
Who desire no pleasure,
  And fear no woe.

The Bells are ringing,
  The sun shines clear,
The Choir is singing,
  The guests are here.
Before the High Altar
  Behold the Bride ;
And a mournful Angel
  Is by her side.
She smiles, all content
  With her chosen lot,—
(Is her last night's dreaming
  So soon forgot ?)
And oh, may the Angel
  Forsake her not !

For on her small hand
There glitters plain
The first sad link
Of a life-long chain ;—
And she needs his guiding
Through paths of pain.

THE ANGEL'S BIDDING.

NOT a sound is heard in the Convent;
    The Vesper Chant is sung,
    The sick have all been tended,
The poor nun's toils are ended
Till the Matin bell has rung.
All is still, save the Clock, that is ticking
So loud in the frosty air,
And the soft snow, falling as gently
As an answer to a prayer.
    But an Angel whispers, " Oh, Sister,
    You must rise from your bed to pray;
    In the silent, deserted chapel,
    You must kneel till the dawn of day;
    For, far on the desolate moorland,
    So dreary, and bleak, and white,
    There is one, all alone and helpless,
    In peril of death to-night.

" No sound on the moorland to guide him,
    No star in the murky air ;
And he thinks of his home and his loved ones
    With the tenderness of despair ;
He has wandered for hours in the snow-drift,
    And he strives to stand in vain,
So lies down to dream of his children,
    And never to rise again.
        Then kneel in the silent chapel
        Till the dawn of to-morrow's sun,
        And ask of the Lord you worship
        For the life of that desolate one ;
        And the smiling eyes of his children
        Will gladden his heart again,
        And the grateful tears of God's poor ones
        Will fall on your soul like rain !—

" Yet, leave him alone to perish,
    And the grace of your God implore,
With all the strength of your spirit,
    For one who needs it more.
Far away, in the gleaming city,
    Amid perfume, and song, and light,
A soul that Jesus has ransomed
    Is in peril of sin to-night.

" The Tempter is close beside him,
    And his danger is all forgot,
And the far-off voices of childhood
    Call aloud, but he hears them not:

He sayeth no prayer, and his mother—
　　He thinks not of her to-day,
And he will not look up to Heaven,
　　And his Angel is turning away.

" Then pray for a soul in peril,
　　A soul for which Jesus died ;
Ask, by the cross that bore Him,
　　And by her who stood beside ;
And the Angels of God will thank you,
　　And bend from their thrones of light,
To tell you that Heaven rejoices
　　At the deed you have done to-night."

SPRING.

HARK! the Hours are softly calling,
　　Bidding Spring arise,
　　To listen to the raindrops falling
　　From the cloudy skies,
To listen to Earth's weary voices,
　　Louder every day,
Bidding her no longer linger
　　On her charmèd way ;
But hasten to her task of beauty
　　Scarcely yet begun ;

Spring.

By the first bright day of summer
    It should all be done.
She has yet to loose the fountain
    From its iron chain ;
And to make the barren mountain
    Green and bright again ;
She must clear the snow that lingers
    Round the stalks away,
And let the snowdrop's trembling whiteness
    See the light of day.
She must watch, and warm, and cherish
    Every blade of green ;
Till the tender grass appearing
    From the earth is seen ;
She must bring the golden crocus
    From her hidden store ;
She must spread broad showers of daisies
    Each day more and more.
In each hedgerow she must hasten
    Cowslips sweet to set ;
Primroses in rich profusion,
    With bright dewdrops wet,
And under every leaf, in shadow
    Hide a Violet !
Every tree within the forest
    Must be decked anew
And the tender buds of promise
    Should be peeping through,
Folded deep, and almost hidden,
    Leaf by leaf beside,

What will make the Summer's glory,
    And the Autumn's pride.
She must weave the loveliest carpets,
    Chequered sun and shade,
Every wood must have such pathways,
    Laid in every glade;
She must hang laburnum branches
    On each archèd bough;—
And the white and purple lilac
    Should be waving now;
She must breathe, and cold winds vanish
    At her breath away;
And then load the air around her
    With the scent of May!
Listen then, Oh Spring! nor linger
    On thy charmèd way;
Have pity on thy prisoned flowers
    Wearying for the day.
Listen to the raindrops falling
    From the cloudy skies;
Listen to the hours calling,
    Bidding thee arise.

EVENING HYMN.

THE shadows of the evening hours
   Fall from the darkening sky;
Upon the fragrance of the flowers
   The dews of evening lie:
Before Thy throne, O Lord of Heaven,
   We kneel at close of day;
Look on Thy children from on high,
   And hear us while we pray.

The sorrows of Thy Servants, Lord,
   Oh, do not Thou despise;
But let the incense of our prayers
   Before Thy mercy rise:
The brightness of the coming night
   Upon the darkness rolls:
With hopes of future glory chase
   The shadows on our souls.

Slowly the rays of daylight fade;
   So fade within our heart,
The hopes in earthly love and joy,
   That one by one depart:
Slowly the bright stars, one by one,
   Within the Heavens shine;—
Give us, Oh Lord, fresh hopes in Heaven,
   And trust in things divine.

A A

Let peace, Oh Lord, Thy peace, Oh God,
  Upon our souls descend ;
From midnight fears and perils, Thou
  Our trembling hearts defend ;
Give us a respite from our toil,
  Calm and subdue our woes ;
Through the long day we suffer, Lord,
  Oh, give us now repose !

THE INNER CHAMBER.

IN the outer Court I was singing,
    Was singing the whole day long ;
  From the inner chamber were ringing
Echoes repeating my song.

And I sang till it grew immortal ;
  For that very song of mine,
When re-echoed behind the Portal,
  Was filled with a life divine.

Was the Chamber a silver round
  Of arches, whose magical art
Drew in coils of musical sound,
  And cast them back on my heart?

Was there hidden within a lyre
  Which, as air breathed over its strings,
Filled my song with a soul of fire,
  And sent back my words with wings?

Was some seraph imprisoned there,
  Whose Voice made my song complete,
And whose lingering, soft despair,
  Made the echo so faint and sweet?

Long I trembled and paused—then parted
  The curtains with heavy fringe;
And, half fearing, yet eager-hearted
  Turned the door on its golden hinge.

Now I sing in the court once more,
  I sing and I weep all day,
As I kneel by the close-shut door,
  For I know what the echoes say.

Yet I sing not the song of old,
  Ere I knew whence the echo came,
Ere I opened the door of gold ;
  But the music sounds just the same.

Then take warning, and turn away;
  Do not ask of that hidden thing.
Do not guess what the echoes say,
  Or the meaning of what I sing.

HEARTS.

I.

A TRINKET made like a Heart, dear,
   Of red gold, bright and fine,
   Was given to me for a keepsake,
Given to me for mine.

And another heart, warm and tender,
   As true as a heart could be;
And every throb that stirred it
   Was always and all for me.

Sailing over the waters,
   Watching the far blue land,
I dropped my golden heart, dear,
   Dropped it out of my hand !

It lies in the cold blue waters,
   Fathoms and fathoms deep,
The golden heart which I promised,
   Promised to prize and keep.

Gazing at Life's bright visions,
   So false, and fair, and new,
I forgot the other heart, dear,
   Forgot it and lost it too !

I might seek that heart for ever,
 I might seek and seek in vain ;-
And for one short, careless hour,
 I pay with a life of pain.

II.

THE Heart ?—Yes, I wore it
 As sign and as token
  Of a love that once gave it,
A vow that was spoken ;
But a love, and a vow, and a heart
 Can be broken.

The Love ?—Life and Death
 Are crushed into a day,
So what wonder that Love
 Should as soon pass away—
What wonder I saw it
 Fade, fail, and decay.

The Vow ?—why what was it,
 It snapped like a thread :
Who cares for the corpse
 When the spirit is fled ?
Then I said, "Let the Dead rise
 And bury its dead,

" While the true, living future
    Grows pure, wise, and strong."
So I cast the gold heart,
    I had worn for so long,
In the Lake, and bound on it
    A Stone—and a Wrong!

III.

LOOK, this little golden Heart
    Was a true-love shrine
    For a tress of hair; I held them,
    Heart and tress, as mine,
Like the Love which gave the token—
See to-day the Heart is broken!

Broken is the golden heart,
    Lost the tress of hair;
Ah, the shrine is empty, vacant,
    Desolate, and bare!
So the token should depart,
When Love dies within the heart.

Fast and deep the river floweth,
    Floweth to the west;
I will cast the golden trinket
    In its cold dark breast,—
Flow, oh river, deep and fast,
Over all the buried past!

TWO LOVES.

DEEP within my heart of hearts, dear,
　　Bound with all its strings,
　Two Loves are together reigning,
　　Both are crowned like Kings ;
While my life, still uncomplaining,
　　Rests beneath their wings.

So they both will rule my heart, dear,
　　'Till it cease to beat ;
No sway can be deeper, stronger,
　　Truer, more complete ;
Growing, as it lasts the longer,
　　Sweeter, and more sweet.

One all life and time transfigures
　　Piercing through and through
Meaner things with magic splendour,
　　Old, yet ever new :
This,—so strong and yet so tender,—
　　Is . . . my Love for you.

Should it fail,—forgive my doubting
　　In this world of pain,—
Yet my other Love would ever
　　Steadfastly remain ;

And I know that I could never
  Turn to that in vain.

Though its radiance may be fainter,
  Yet its task is wide ;
For it lives to comfort sorrows,
  Strengthen, calm, and guide,
And from Trust and Honour borrows
  All its peace and pride.

Will you blame my dreaming, even
  If the first were flown ?
Ah, I would not live without it,
  It is all your own :
And the other—can you doubt it ?—
  Yours, and yours alone.

A WOMAN'S LAST WORD.

WELL—the links are broken,
    All is past ;
  This farewell, when spoken,
    Is the last.
I have tried and striven
    All in vain ;

Such bonds must be riven,
    Spite of pain,
And never, never, never
    Knit again.

So I tell you plainly,
    It must be :
I shall try, not vainly,
    To be free ;
Truer, happier chances
    Wait me yet,
While you, through fresh fancies,
    Can forget ;—
And life has nobler uses
    Than Regret.

All past words retracing,
    One by one,
Does not help effacing
    What is done.
Let it be. Oh, stronger
    Links can break !
Had we dreamed still longer
    We could wake,—
Yet let us part in kindness
    For Love's sake.

Bitterness and sorrow
    Will at last,
In some bright to-morrow,
    Heal their past ;

But future hearts will never
　　　Be as true
As mine was—is ever,
　　　Dear, for you . . . . .
　. Then must we part, when loving
　　　As we do?

PAST AND PRESENT.

"LINGER," I cried, "oh radiant Time! thy power
　　　Has nothing more to give; life is complete:
Let but the perfect Present, hour by hour,
Itself remember and itself repeat.

"And Love,—the future can but mar its splendour,
Change can but dim the glory of its youth;
Time has no star more faithful or more tender,
To crown its constancy or light its truth."

But Time passed on in spite of prayer or pleading,
Through storm and peril; but that life might gain
A Peace through strife all other peace exceeding,
Fresh joy from sorrow, and new hope from pain.

And since Love lived when all save Love was dying,
And, passed through fire, grew stronger than before:—
Dear, you know why, in double faith relying,
I prize the Past much, but the Present more.

FOR THE FUTURE.

WONDER did you ever count
   The value of one human fate,
Or sum the infinite amount
   Of one heart's treasures, and the weight
Of Life's one venture, and the whole concentrate
    purpose of a soul.

And if you ever paused to think
   That all this in your hands I laid
Without a fear :—did you not shrink
   From such a burthen ? half afraid,
Half wishing that you could divide the risk, or cast it
    all aside.

While Love has daily perils, such
   As none foresee and none control ;
And hearts are strung so that one touch,
   Careless or rough, may jar the whole,
You well might feel afraid to reign with absolute
    power of joy and pain.

You well might fear—if Love's sole claim
   Were to be happy : but true Love
Takes joy as solace, not as aim,
   And looks beyond, and looks above ;
And sometimes through the bitterest strife first learns
    to live her highest life.

Earth forges joy into a chain
Till fettered Love forgets its strength,
Its purpose, and its end ;—but Pain
Restores its heritage at length,
And bids Love rise again and be eternal, mighty, pure,
    and free.

If then your future life should need
A strength my Love can only gain
Through suffering, or my heart be freed
Only by sorrow, from some stain—
Then you shall give, and I will take, this Crown of fire
    for Love's dear sake.

Sept. 8th, 1860.

CHISWICK PRESS :—C. WHITTINGHAM AND CO., TOOKS COURT,
CHANCERY LANE.

www.ingramcontent.com/pod-product-compliance
Lightning Source LLC
Chambersburg PA
CBHW021531110726
47902CB00004B/830